Hidden in the coal bin, Anne prayed that he would not turn toward her. . . .

She realized his true intention only when he threw back the furnace door and stoked the fire with savage satisfaction.

What was it that he threw into the flames? Sticks of kindling? Shreds of cloth?

Or was it the thing her mind refused to acknowledge?

The cellar was stifling. She gagged as she turned from the searing heat.

She was trapped in a grim inferno.

**THE HOUSE AT CANTERBURY**
is an original POCKET BOOK edition.

Books by Fortune Kent

The House at Canterbury
Isle of the Seventh Sentry

Published by POCKET BOOKS

# The
# *House at*
# *Canterbury*

## by Fortune Kent

PUBLISHED BY POCKET BOOKS NEW YORK

THE HOUSE AT CANTERBURY

POCKET BOOK edition published October, 1975

Standard Book Number: 671-80196-1.

# The
# House at
# Canterbury

# Chapter 1

I suffer a recurring dream in which I am lost in a house of many rooms.

I walk along hushed corridors, climb spiral stairs to towers with windows boarded in a strange geometry, descend to cellars pungent with the fumes of coal stored to fuel fires in black furnaces.

Scents from the past torment me: burning leaves, rotted planks in summerhouse sanctuaries, the tang of clothes laid on radiators to dry, wisps of forgotten yesterdays.Voices murmur from behind the walls, enticing me to rooms bereft of windows. Clocks tick on mantels above empty fireplaces. The whispers beckon, but always from beyond.

I face a choice of doors. Only a seeming choice, for my hand moves as though predestined. My fingers grip the knob, my heart pounds expectantly, as I envision candlelight in an opulent suite where a lover waits, impatient for me to join him. The door opens on a barren hall. Ahead I see a cul-de-sac and more choices already foreordained. Behind me the door thuds shut with the finality of death.

Sounds rise from all the corridors not taken. Men and women laugh, weep. "Anne, Anne," they call. I run, but my feet move with a maddening slowness. The voices reverberate, echo in my mind. The music of a dance band swells in a familiar melody and I hum the tune—yet the words elude me. The music ends with a spatter of applause. I reach for the cathedral-shaped radio, twist the dial and the announcer's voice recedes, clicks off.

As I hover between sleep and waking the babble returns. From all about I hear moans of passion, cries of pain. A scream slices into my consciousness, a wail of frustration, rage and fear. The scream is mine. . . .

I woke up trembling in the early morning stillness of my room. The luminous dial read one twenty-five. I lay on my stomach with my toes over the edge of the mattress while I drew deep breaths and tried to make my mind blank. Ten, nine, eight, seven, six, I counted. To no avail.

Why couldn't I will myself to sleep? "You're an excellent subject," the hypnotist had told me. I had returned a second night and watched him hypnotize another woman as he had me. "When you hear 'Smoke Gets in Your Eyes,'" he said, "you will give your husband a passionate kiss, the most passionate kiss you have ever given him in your life. . . ."

I turned onto my side. Phantoms crept into my mind with their messages of apprehension. Was he home? Across the room the flat outline of his bed answered no. I swung my feet to the floor and buttoned my robe as I shivered in the chill night of September in California.

I groped along the hall, for I had not yet mastered the geography of our condominium. The silent switch lighted an apartment with all the personality of a problem in trigonometry. I enjoyed trig problems—found them logical, precise, sterile. I liked the apartment.

The stereo? No, I decided—music led only one way, to the past. When sleep wouldn't come I worked crossword puzzles, read poetry, or skimmed improbable novels. A dust jacket heralding a turbulent saga of three generations always tempted me—perhaps because I was an only child, or because generations would not follow me. We had no children.

I opened a book of poems and felt the pricks of smiles catch in my skin like little hooks. Sylvia Plath—one of the first myths of the Women's Movement, a martyr found with her head in a gas oven. Refrigerators, sinks, toilet bowls and cooking stoves. The symbols of our discontent.

I laid the book two inches from the top of the coffee table, two inches from the side. Now I was wide awake. Twenty minutes before two. I felt taut, my anxiety mixed with resentment and fear. Did I hear his car? Did a door slam? I hurried through the kitchen and looked into the garage. No bulk of an automobile, nothing.

Back in the living room I avoided the stereo on my way to the window. I pulled the cord and the drapes slid open to frame the lights of the city far below. An alien city on an alien shore. A sere land so unlike the green of the Hudson Valley, where year after year the seasons repeated the rhythm of life and death.

Ten minutes before two. "Hell," I said aloud. I turned on the stereo and stared at the record revolving on the turntable. What was the condescending phrase? "Oldies but goodies." Why can't they at least give us *"and* goodies" instead of insisting on the "but"?

"Seven," the male vocalist sang. "We leave at seven," he said, "for a sentimental journey." One of the songs from the last year of the war. After I danced a few steps the thick carpet discouraged me. My dream, almost forgotten, came back like an echo no less painful for being familiar. The rooms in the dream were the rooms of the house in Canterbury, the voices those of Jeremy, his father, Don, all the others—and the fear was the fear I had known then.

I lay on the couch and shut my eyes and, as though the music triggered an hypnotic suggestion, I again saw the village of Canterbury with the trees arched over the streets, the school with row on row of windows, the clock in the classroom edging back before snapping forward, the two houses (mine and the Blackstock place), the river beyond the trees, the mountain in the distance.

The face of the mountain dropped precipitously from the summit to the river. Halfway down, the highway had been cut into the cliff like a notch carved into the stock of an outlaw's rifle.

*Three were dead, not one. Where were the other two notches?*

I twisted on the couch. The past can't wound me anymore, I thought. I bunched the pillow beneath my head. Almost thirty years ago and I remembered as if it were only yesterday. Where had everything begun to go awry? Was there a signal I had missed?

"Don't go to Canterbury," Karl had said. "You'll be alone, hundreds of miles away. Don't go."

"I have to," I told him. "Father gave me the house," I added, as if that fact explained all.

The paperboy. Was he the first warning? Or was there something even earlier, back home, before I went to Canterbury? The umbrellas slick in the rain, the smell of dark wet earth, the long line of black cars parked at the bottom of the hill.

I had been close to my father and now he was dead. Yes, death at the beginning and later, in Canterbury, death, unnatural death, at the ending . . .

# Chapter 2

I drove the black '42 Dodge through the morning mist toward Canterbury. I liked the sound, Canterbury, for it reminded me of stories from my childhood of knights rescuing maidens from forbidden towers. I now repeated the name of my new home like an incantation, for in Canterbury I would free myself from the numbness that had followed my father's death.

Instead of feeling uneasy when I couldn't find Canterbury on my map, I was pleased. A small secluded town appealed to me, for I had been, when younger, a girl who exchanged secret messages written in lemon juice, a girl who sought refuge in wooded glens. I dreamed of a new beginning in this remote village on the Hudson where a house waited for me, a gift from my father a few months before he died. And next week I was to begin teaching mathematics at the high school. I felt a tingle of excitement, of anticipation mingled with apprehension, for I would be, I knew, alone in a village of strangers.

I turned left and noticed that the mist had lifted,

but heavy clouds threatened rain. Woods, looking out of place this close to Manhattan, huddled on both sides of the highway. The leaves were turning and an occasional maple was radiantly red, orange and yellow, a preview of the Technicolor spectacular to come. The year, I thought, must die to be reborn.

To my right I caught glimpses of the river, grey and bleak. A few drops of water spotted the windshield and I slowed, expecting the rain to start, yet it did not. I might still reach Canterbury before the storm broke.

Smoke drifted across the highway, bringing the smell of burning leaves, and suddenly, unexpectedly, I was homesick. Am I making a mistake? I wondered. Should I have left the home I had known for years? But the memories of my father were too vivid there.

"I'm tired of lawyers and their talk of debts," I had told Karl. "I need a new beginning." Now, only a few miles from Canterbury, I wasn't sure.

At West Point a soldier barred my way. "The military academy has been closed to visitors since the start of the war," he told me as he directed me to a detour. I felt a shock, not unpleasant, as though the war had touched me personally. Every innocent-looking driver of a passing car became a disguised Nazi plotting to penetrate West Point's defenses.

After circling the perimeter of the academy, I drove along the side of a mountain high above the river. Rounding a promontory, I saw another mountain loom ahead with the highway cut into its face like a notch on the blade of a paring knife. The sky grew dark and a few large drops of rain made starlike bursts on my windshield. The wind rose, tossing the tops of the trees, gusting rain at the car. Squalls obscured the mountains on the far side of the river.

I turned on the wipers, peered through the water streaming over the windshield at dim yellow lights warning of approaching cars, slowed, heard the tires of the other cars hiss past on the wet pavement. I noticed a turnoff and, at the last minute, swung my car from the road, stopped and switched off the motor. Should I have left it running? Would the water flood the engine? Rain throbbed on the roof with an insistent beat. The windows fogged over. I folded my arms and hunched into the corner between seat and door. When I tell him, I thought, Father will laugh at my fears.

"Don't worry, princess," he'll say, "everything will turn out for the best." My throat tightened with shock when I realized I had forgotten he was dead. I was alone.

The inside of the car was humid and perspiration gathered on my face. I wiped my forehead with a handkerchief, then used the cloth to clean a square on the window, but I could see nothing except slanting lines of rain. Once more the glass misted. Marooned high on the mountainside, cut off from the world, I felt imprisoned. Like the heroine of a fairy tale, I thought.

At last the storm slackened so I could roll down the window. Water splashed my cheek. I turned the key, heard the motor grind and die. Tense, I tried again. I pressed gently on the gas and the car started. I sighed. When the wiper swished the water from the windshield I saw a low stone wall separating me from a cliff that dropped hundreds of feet to the whitecap-flecked river. A tug steamed downstream with a string of barges in tow. Clouds shrouded the mountains on the far shore, but in the sky above I saw a wedge of blue.

I eased the car back onto the cement pavement and, keeping well under the thirty-mile speed limit, followed the twisting road away from the river along the mountain's edge. I passed a few houses, an inn set back beneath elms, a sign proclaiming VILLAGE OF CANTERBURY— POPULATION: 2,100. The wipers slapped and squealed until I turned them off. The storm was over.

What awaited me here? I wondered. Anne Medford, number 2,101. I had never been to Canterbury. In 1939, on my only trip to New York, my father and I had decided to spend an extra day at the World's Fair rather than journey north to see the house.

I took deep breaths of air freshened by rain. What an attractive town, I thought, seeing the trees arch over the quiet streets. I passed the Canterbury High School, a three-story brick building with row on row of windows. My school. The walkways were deserted, but on the playground boys threw a football back and forth. Would I get along with boys like these? I knew they could make a new teacher's life a joy or a hell. What would they think of Miss Anne Medford, mathematics teacher?

I was used to hearing people say, "You're too pretty to be a math teacher." How do math teachers look? Must they be men with creased faces wearing rumpled suits streaked with chalk dust?

"You don't act like a math teacher," they said. "Math teachers are precise and logical." Precise? Well, perhaps I wasn't precise, but I was willing to defend my logic.

Would I be a good teacher? I wanted to teach. Not because I liked mathematics, although I did, nor because I thought I could help others learn, though I hoped I could. And not just because my mother, who died when I was nine, had been a teacher. My reason for becoming a teacher was uncomplicated. I liked young people.

A short way past the school five streets met to form the center of the village. I saw a drug store, a movie theater, a bar. A blue-and-white New York-bound bus was stopped across the street and several men and women were climbing aboard. In front of a combination restaurant/bar old men with furled umbrellas stood talking—of other days and other storms, I supposed.

I stopped for gas at Quinlan's Service Station. While the attendant, a short white-haired man, checked the oil and water, I got out to stretch. In the rest room I combed my hair and put on lipstick. I looked at my reflection. Wistfully I compared myself to my mother as I remembered her—her hair had been blonde, mine was brown; she was petite, slightly over five feet, while I was three inches taller, an in-between height; her complexion had been fair while mine still displayed remnants of the freckles that plagued me as a child.

When I came outside the car was ready. I surrendered the last of my precious A-ration coupons and paid for the gas. "Can you tell me how to get to Spruce Street?" I asked. I couldn't keep the anticipation from my voice.

"Spruce? Go up the hill to the Heights, then straight ahead for three blocks. It's the last street before you come to the bluff above the river."

As I waited to turn onto the highway I noticed, next to the gas station, a flag hanging limply in front of a three-panelled display board, the CANTERBURY HONOR ROLL. Most of the name plaques nailed to the board were lettered in black, but a few were gold. Black meant life while gold was the color of death. I frowned and looked away.

I drove to the Heights where the streets had been named for trees—Elm, Maple, Hickory. Spruce Street, its macadam surface black from the rain, was bordered by two rows of evergreens. Old, spacious homes sat comfortably in large yards. I had pictured my house as being on a street just like this.

I recalled what my father had told me about the house. "Your mother and I went to Canterbury on vacation," he said. "She fell in love with the village and the house." The price had been low and, intending either to refurbish and resell, or to keep the house rented and eventually return to live in Canterbury, my father had bought it. The Depression intervened and nothing was done.

How like one of my father's plans, I thought. He dreamed, he always dreamed; yet he had never been able to make his dreams come true, not completely. He would have, I thought, if he had had more time. His last business was just getting out of the red when he died. All he needed was more time.

"We've a good tenant in the house," my father said. "A Mrs. Allison who lives downstairs." He smiled. "One word of warning: seems there's a local feeling against the place. You know what small towns are like. Let a big house stand vacant a few years and the townspeople think ghosts move in."

I smiled to myself. Ghosts? No, no ghosts—this was 1944. Besides, I had plans for the house that would put any ghosts to flight.

I looked on both sides of the street for number eleven and found a tarnished "89" on a post next to a driveway on the river side, but I could see no other numbers. I passed a boy with a newspaper-carrier's bag slung over one shoulder so I slowed, intending to ask directions—but he turned into a yard without seeing me. None of the next few houses had numbers. Giving up, I pulled to the side of the road in front of a high white fence.

When I slid from my car the paperboy was coming toward me, going from house to house on the other side of the street tossing folded papers onto front porches. I waited beside the Dodge. The boy, who looked about fifteen, was tall, freckled and wore glasses. As he approached he held a folded paper so it slap-slap-slapped on the fence. An unusual fence, I thought, as high as my head, with not two but four horizontal rails and thick, square pickets spiked on the top. A gate was flanked by a pair of wooden columns crowned by urns from which vines twisted their way to the ground. The boy inserted the folded paper between the gate and one of the columns. When he saw me he stopped.

"Do you know which house is number eleven?" I asked. He stared blankly.

"I don't know the numbers," he said. "We don't use numbers."

"The Medford house." He shook his head. "Where Mrs. Allison lives," I added.

He smiled. "Oh, you mean the old Lorch place. This here is Blackstocks' "—he indicated the white fence—"the next is where Mrs. Allison lives"—he pointed back the way he had come. The next house. I was almost there.

"Thank you," I said. He nodded and went on. I debated taking the car, but decided to walk. Inside the Blackstocks' fence the leaves had been raked into piles and the shrubs trimmed. A path led from the gate to a row of pines planted only a few feet apart to form a barrier so thick I couldn't see the house.

I reached the post at the end of the yard where the fence made a right angle and continued along the side

of the estate to disappear down a long slope. To the
rear I saw the tops of trees and the river in the distance.

Next door a drive led from the street past a tangle
of barberries into my yard. *My* yard. *My* house at Canterbury. Through overgrown shrubs I saw the building,
as grey as the sky. My first impression was of wide
porches, peaked roofs and tall chimneys. The only houses
I could see on the river side were mine and the Blackstocks'.

I looked back, wondered again whether to go for
the car and watched the paperboy, far down the street
now, unlatch a gate and walk to another front porch.
I pursed my lips. Something was wrong; a subtle difference nagged at me. What was the inconsistency? The
street? No. The Blackstock place? No.

Wait, the paperboy. Yes, something the boy had done
or failed to do. I reviewed his actions from the time
I had first seen him. Then I knew. Only at the Blackstocks', of all the houses on the street, had he thrust the
newspaper into the gate instead of entering the yard to
throw it on the porch. Why?

Was Charles Blackstock a recluse? I tried to recall
if I had heard of anything to account for his evident
desire for seclusion, but could not. I knew he did repair
work for my father. "He's retired," Father had said,
"lives next door, doesn't seem to need the money, but
likes to keep busy. I think he used to be a carpenter."

As I turned to enter my driveway I was startled by
a crunching of gravel and a sharp yelp. I looked up
to see a lean black-and-brown dog, a Doberman pinscher,
lope down the Blackstocks' walk and leap to place both
front paws on the top rail of the gate. I gasped. Panting,
he looked about, jumped to the ground and raced along
the inside of the fence toward me. I backed away. He
crouched, snarling, then threw himself at the white
pickets.

I shut my eyes, a scream rising in my throat. The
dog's lithe body thudded on the fence and he whined,
scraping the wood with his claws. The barberry tore the

backs of my legs and I opened my eyes to see the dog thrusting his snout at the top of the fence, head between the points of the pickets, teeth bared.

"Down, Brutus, down!" A sharp, commanding voice. The dog dropped to the ground. A tall man dressed in black trousers, a black pullover and a white shirt open at the neck strode toward me. His face was set and cold.

The dog trotted to him and nuzzled against his leg. The man fondled the dog, rubbed his ears, smiled, then walked to the fence where he placed both hands on the rail and leaned forward, his brown eyes staring at me, the smile gone. For a moment I met his gaze; I saw a full dark face and long wavy black hair. Although grey showed at his temples he couldn't have been more than thirty, too young to be Charles Blackstock.

"What are you doing?" he demanded. My eyes dropped.

"Doing?"

"Didn't you see the sign?" I shook my head, glancing up as he frowned. What can you expect? his look said.

I'll be damned if I'll let you intimidate me, I thought. "I'm Anne Medford," I told him. "Your new neighbor."

His eyes widened, but I couldn't read his expression. "Jeremy," he said at last. "Jeremy Blackstock." The dog whined at his feet until Jeremy patted his head. Without another word he turned and strode back toward his house. I stared after him.

I trembled as I watched the dog trot behind his master. I was frightened of the dog and frustrated by Jeremy Blackstock's abruptness. When my trembling stopped I walked on between the puddles on the drive. My drive. I looked across to the Blackstocks' and saw that Jeremy had paused in the shadows of the pines. I thought he watched me, but I couldn't be sure.

I kicked a pebble hard and it bounced through the weeds to splash into a pool of water. I was calmer now—calm and angry. Jeremy had been arrogant and overbearing. Jeremy. I said his name to myself: Jeremy Blackstock.

I glanced again toward the pines, saw the branches heavy with rain, the lengthening shadows, nothing more. He was gone.

# Chapter 3

I turned away from the Blackstock grounds, away from Jeremy Blackstock. His rudeness had been uncalled for. Still, could I have done something to cause his hostility? Stop, I told myself. Anne, you begin by placing the blame where it belongs—on your boorish neighbor—and end by questioning yourself. He had no right to be curt; you have no reason to feel guilty.

No man had ever been as brusque to me as Jeremy had. Sometimes men were put off by my being a math major; they are, I've found, suspicious of any woman able to do even the simple arithmetic necessary to balance a bankbook. But usually I get along with men. Because I like them, I suppose.

There are girls that boys ask to go with them to study in the library and girls that they ask to the junior prom. I was more the library kind. By boys I mean those you really want to go to the prom with. After awhile I came to believe some girls were born with a quality I lacked, an innate ability to play up to men, a coquettishness. My mistake with men was in always being myself, but that seemed the only way I could be.

"Anne, you're naïve where men are concerned," my college roommate had told me.

When I'd repeated her remark to my father he'd laughed. "Don't worry, princess," he'd said, "you're being smart, not naïve. Be patient—the right man will come along, and when he does, you'll be glad you waited."

At times I'd wondered how long I would have to wait, especially when I found myself becoming more immersed in Advanced Calculus 472 and Educational Theory 104 than I wanted to be. Until Karl. I'd met Karl in one of my required science courses. He was a physics major. Last March, to my surprise and probably his as well, Karl had asked me to marry him. Although he was all a girl might wish for—good-looking, intelligent, pleasant—still I'd felt an indefinable uneasiness, a hesitation. I'd told him I wasn't sure, that marriage wouldn't work unless we both were sure. But we'd kept seeing each other.

I owed a great deal to Karl, yet now he was at Camp Blanding in Florida while I was in Canterbury. And all because of last summer, because of my fears, my uncertainties.

Birds screeched at me from the overgrown shrubs that obscured my view of the house. A bluejay strutted across the leaf-strewn lawn. I shook my head. I didn't want to think about what had happened last summer.

As I walked between the shrubs I saw a flash of orange from my house and I stopped, thinking for a moment that the building was on fire. Then I realized light from the setting sun had slanted between a rift in the clouds to glint on the upstairs windows. In a few seconds the glass was blank again, and when I looked behind me only the sun's rim shone above the clouds.

The nearer I came to the house the more uneasy I felt. I knew what I had expected, what I had dreamed the house should be—a romantic mansion of towers, gables and a multitude of chimneys; a charming Victorian monstrosity glowering over lawns that sloped to the lapping waters of the Hudson.

The house was all this. Yet for an instant the disrepair filled me with dismay: the lack of paint, the roof whose tinplated shingles were stained with rust, the porch littered with twigs and dead branches, the gutters clogged with sodden leaves. Loose bricks made the two front chimneys tilt precariously. Brown and desiccated ivy clung to the weathered clapboards, while the same plants sent green tendrils crawling over the lawn.

The house seemed so vulnerable, so defenseless.

Perhaps because of the decay or the many windows or the absence of protecting trees. I remembered a former neighbor, old Mr. McGowan, who'd lived to be one hundred and three. His friends gone, his children dead, he'd found himself regarded as a curiosity, admired by people who'd never known him—admired not for what he was or what he had been, but because he had managed to survive.

I had planned on a few months of work turning my relic into a castle. Now, realizing the magnitude of the task, I sighed, wishing I could share my feeling of discouragement with my father, as I had shared so many of my problems in the past. I climbed the porch steps and pushed the bell. A chime sounded inside the house.

The door opened at once and a small birdlike woman smiled at me. "I'm Mrs. Allison," she said. "Edith Allison. You must be Anne Medford." She had answered the bell so quickly I wondered if she had watched my approach through one of the glass panels along the sides of the entrance.

"Yes," I said. "I'm glad to meet you."

"You'll have to speak a little louder. I'm a touch hard of hearing." I couldn't place her slight accent.

"Yes. I'm Anne Medford," I said, trying to make each word distinct.

"Come in. I've been expecting you." She held the door open. "The major wants me to get a hearing aid, but I can't abide them. They hurt my ears."

Mrs. Allison's bedroom slippers padded across the front hall, white cottontail puffs bobbing on the toes. Her blue housedress came well below her knees. The hall was gloomy; there was an unlit chandelier over our heads, and unlit bulbs sat in brackets along the walls. A massive mirrored coatrack hulked to one side, a stair curved to the upper floors on the other. A grandfather clock ticked in a recess under the stairs.

"You're going to have supper with me," Mrs. Allison said—I couldn't think of her as Edith. When I started to protest she shook her head. "No, no, you must. I have the meal almost ready. I just have to cook the peas."

Her thin face was pale and sparrowlike. She wore glasses. No, glasses was the wrong word. Spectacles. A fine-mesh net held her grey hair tightly to her head.

Mrs. Allison led me through a dining room to an enormous kitchen. She tied an apron about her waist, then lit one of the burners on the gas range and placed a pan of peas on top. A white cat came from beneath the table, stretched and curled about my legs.

Mrs. Allison scooped him into her arms. "No, no, General," she scolded as she dropped the cat outside the door. "The young lady probably doesn't like cats."

"But I do. I had a cat at home."

"I only have two now," she said. "MacArthur whom you just saw, and Tojo." She smiled. "The major named them."

"The major?"

"My son. He's in the army, stationed near Boston. You might meet him. He thinks he'll get leave soon." At last I realized what her accent was—Scottish.

"When I came in just now I met a young man next door. I wondered why he isn't in the service."

"That horrible dog," she said. So, I thought, amused, she *had* been watching. "Someone should report his dog. Don't be frightened, though. He can't get out of the yard."

"I'm glad of that."

"He can't jump the fence, and they keep the gates locked all the time. But you were asking me about Jeremy. He was in the army for quite a spell, but he's been home almost a year now." She lowered her voice. "I don't know why they discharged him. I don't think he was wounded. Something psychological, they say."

I murmured a noncommittal reply. Shell shock? What do they call it now? Yes, battle fatigue. That would explain why he was prematurely grey. Jeremy Blackstock, I thought, a beribboned World War II veteran, world-weary and cynical, living with his father in his ancestral home in Canterbury, friendless and alone.

"You most likely want to see the rest of your house," Mrs. Allison said. "Do you have any plans for it?"

"Yes, I do. I'll have repairs made if I can find a handyman; do some modernizing, though I'll try to preserve the Victorian decor."

"Oh," she said, sounding hurt. "I do so like living here. I have the lower floor to myself, so I hope you won't want the whole house right away. Of course you're welcome to use the parlor or the phone till you get yours."

"The second floor will do me nicely for now," I said. Should I have mentioned my plans to Mrs. Allison? She seemed so crestfallen. I should have considered the possibility that she might have grown attached to the house.

Mrs. Allison directed me to a stair leading from the far side of the kitchen. "I didn't clean," she said over her shoulder. "I don't like to be one who interferes." The steps were high and about two feet wide, with a wall on both sides.

On the second floor Mrs. Allison opened doors to high-ceilinged rooms in which grey dust covers were spread over the furniture: four bedrooms, a bathroom with a tub sitting on clawlike legs and a tiny kitchen.

"This used to be a sewing room, I'm told," Mrs. Allison said, "but it's been a kitchen since before my time, and I've lived here going on four years. The house is almost a hundred years old. Haunted, they say. What nonsense! All because John Lorch lived here back in 1910 or so and was murdered, or so the story goes. Not here—in New York. I don't know what happened. Don't want to know if the truth be told."

After looking in each of the rooms I led Mrs. Allison back to a large bedroom at the front of the house. An empty gunrack stood beside the door. Across the hall was a closed door with the key in the lock. "The attic," Mrs. Allison explained. "I went up last week, but you have to go during the day if you want to see anything. The light's out."

I opened the bedroom door and when I flicked the switch only two of the bulbs in the chandelier went on. In the dim light I saw a fireplace, washbasins with exposed plumbing, French doors to the balcony on the roof of the porch and large windows facing the front and one side of the house.

"This will be my bedroom," I said. When Mrs. Allison didn't answer I turned and found her still standing in the hall with her hand on the door frame. "Is something the matter?" I asked.

She moved hesitantly into the room, smoothing nonexistent wrinkles from her apron. "No, nothing." She gave a sidelong glance into the dark corners. "Just a feeling," she said. "Sometimes I get feelings about places. Not like my mother who had second sight—just notions I can't explain. Foolish of me, but this room gives me the shivers. I always feel I'm being watched when I'm in here."

I began folding down the cover on the bed. "I don't believe in ghosts," I said.

"Nor do I." Her hand went to her thin mouth. "Oh," she said, "my peas."

"I left my car in front of the Blackstocks'," I told her. "Will I have time to bring it here before supper? Do we have a garage?"

"No, no garage. You have plenty of time. We won't eat for a good twenty minutes." I heard her slippers pad along the hall toward the back stairs.

My pale, tired face stared back from the glass of one of the windows. With no drapes or curtains to shield me from the outside I felt exposed, so I hunched my shoulders and folded my arms across my chest. I turned off the lights. Through a window I could see the spiked tops of the pines and in their midst the Blackstock house, rectangular and squat, silhouetted against the darkening sky. One light from a downstairs window fell over the lawn. Below the house the river was grey in the twilight.

I combed my hair in the bathroom before going down the front stairs. The door to the dining room was open and I looked through to the kitchen, but Mrs. Allison was nowhere to be seen. Once outside on the drive, which circled in front of the house, I hurried, for the evening was cool. Gravel crunched beneath my feet and crickets chirped from the grass around me.

The glow from a streetlight shone dully on the black Dodge. Peering closely I saw a small sign on the Blackstock fence: BEWARE OF THE DOG. I fumbled in my purse until I felt the square end of my key. The car started at once and I pulled from the side of the street. Oh, oh, I thought, something's wrong, for the car bumped. I stopped, got out and walked to the back. The right rear tire was flat.

"Damn," I said under my breath. I took my traveling case from the back seat, locked the doors of the Dodge and trudged to the house. By the time I got the bag into the front hall my arm had begun to ache.

I heard a noise that seemed to come from below. Looking about I saw a door under the stairs next to the grandfather clock—a door I hadn't noticed before, so closely did the wood paneling match the wall. Opening the door I discovered steps leading down into darkness. From below came a clatter and a squeal.

I tiptoed down the stairs. The cellar was not completely dark; shadows wavered on the wall to my right as though a light was swinging from a cord on the far side of the room. A heavy, musty odor made me swallow to keep from coughing.

At the bottom of the stairs I was able to see into the cellar. I gasped. Light flickered on a man's white hair and made his face glow red. Who was he? What was he doing? Not seeing me, he turned and seized a shovel from the wall, pushed it with a great rattling noise into a bin, brought back a shovelful of coal and thrust the fuel into a hissing fire. Heat pulsed from the furnace in the center of the basement. The furnace was a black and hulking monster whose pipes angled along the ceiling of the room.

Since he still hadn't noticed me in the shadows I retreated quietly up the stairs. I found Mrs. Allison in the kitchen scurrying from the refrigerator to the stove to the table.

"There's a man shoveling coal into the furnace," I told her.

"Oh, that's Mr. Blackstock from next door. He takes care of the fire for us."

She sat across from me and I had a forkful of tunafish salad halfway to my mouth before I realized she had bowed her head and clasped her hands in her lap. "I always say grace," she told me, "even when I'm alone." She murmured a brief prayer.

"I found I have a flat tire," I said.

"Oh, dear, you must have picked up a nail on your trip. Don't fret, though. You can get the young man to come over from Quinlan's in the morning. They're real good about that sort of thing."

"Luckily I don't have to go to school tomorrow," I said. "The day after, though, there's a meeting for all the teachers."

"Your picture was in the *Canterbury Local* last week. We have so many new teachers this year because of the draft and others going into war work." She poured the coffee, strong and hot, the way I liked it. "Is this your first year teaching?" she asked.

"Yes. I graduated from Teachers' College last June."

"Only a few men are left this year. Not that there were many before the war either. More men should go into teaching."

"The salaries are too low," I said, thinking of my twenty-two hundred dollars a year.

"I suppose so. You won't find hardly any young men at all around the village these days."

Why did everyone think all young female teachers were looking for husbands? Probably, I thought, because most of them were. Was I? No, not looking, but if the right man happened to come along . . .

"The war." Mrs. Allison shook her head as she stirred sugar into her coffee. "Seems like the war will never end."

"It should be over soon."

"Three years now. I remember when the Japs bombed Pearl Harbor. 'We'll win in a few weeks,' everyone said.

Then last year after we landed in Italy—" She held a handkerchief to her face. Was she crying? " 'Only a few months more,' they said." She sipped her coffee. "All the boys are gone and who knows if they'll ever come back—and even if they do what will they be like after all they're going through? Look at Jeremy Blackstock."

"He seemed all right to me. He was rude, yes, but not odd or strange."

Again she shook her head. "Those Blackstocks, there's bad blood in that family. A taint. Not on the father's side. The mother's. She was an Abbott. If this were the old country—my mother came from Scotland, from Paisley where they make the Paisley pattern—they'd say a curse was on the Abbotts." When she talked of Scotland, Mrs. Allison's burr became more distinct.

"Old Mrs. Abbott, Jeremy's grandmother, seemed all right, they say, though at times she was a mite moody and depressed. Then one August afternoon she walked into the river for no apparent reason. Just walked in till the water covered her. They found her hat, one of those floppy, broad-brimmed kind, floating on the water. Her body didn't wash ashore for three days.

"The father, Charles, now he's different. He's a fine upstanding gentleman even if he is a German. Does other work here in the house besides looking after the furnace. But his son, Jeremy, I don't know about him." Her voice trailed off.

"What do you mean?" I asked.

"Nothing you can put your finger on. A good-looking boy, almost handsome you might say, in a dark way, though I wish he'd get his hair cut more often. Takes after his mother's side of the family. I see him walking in the evenings along the bluff over the river. Moody, he is, and writes with both hands."

"What? You mean he's ambidextrous?"

"No, more than that. He can take two sheets of paper and write two letters at the same time, each different, one with his right hand, the other with his left. It's not natural to be like that. It's as though the two sides of his nature were fighting for control."

"I don't think . . ."

"A shame it is," Mrs. Allison went on, "and not his fault, I suppose. The sins of the fathers like the Bible says. The mothers in this case."

Mrs. Allison started to clear away the dishes. "Let me help," I said. "Does he have a mother then? Living, I mean."

"Just stack them in the sink. It's time for Lowell Thomas. I never miss Lowell Thomas."

We walked into a living room furnished with bookcases, floor lamps and overstuffed chairs. Mrs. Allison turned the knob of a cathedral-shaped radio and we waited while the set warmed up.

*Good evening, everybody.*

"Just in time," Mrs. Allison said, as she settled back in the easy chair beside the radio.

The war news was good. American troops had advanced in the Low Countries, Moscow communiqués reported victories in the Balkans and U.S. planes had bombed the Ruhr again.

"What did you mean about the sins of—" I started to ask when the commercial began.

Mrs. Allison held up her hand. "When this is over," she said.

Lowell Thomas returned to report a slow start in the presidential campaign—Dewey and Bricker running against Roosevelt and Truman. Mrs. Allison didn't turn the radio off until the end of the fifteen-minute program.

"Truman!" she said. "I never heard of him before the convention. The Blackstocks?" she asked. "You wanted to know more about the Blackstocks?"

I nodded. Why do I? I asked myself. I'm not usually one who listens to gossip.

"The mother, I understand, was a real pretty woman," Mrs. Allison said. "I never laid eyes on her myself, of course, since I've only been in Canterbury eight years, but he's shown me pictures of her. Pale with dark hair. Now I think of it, she looked a bit like you. Nobody knows why he put up with her all those years. Charles, her husband, I mean. But he did. She ran around with other men."

"Is she dead?"

"No. She left bag and baggage some eleven or twelve years ago with one of her men friends—a stranger who was here trying to organize the men at the carpet mill. They went on strike all right, were out eight weeks; then they had to go back without getting what they wanted. The next week she and the man ran off and no one's seen her since, though Mr. Blackstock's heard from her. Chicago they went to. But he'd had enough and never tried to get her back. Good riddance to bad rubbish, I say."

"And Jeremy?"

"He was young then, of course. In high school. Turned him against women, seems like. A shame. I can't understand a mother who'd do a thing like that."

"Nor can I." I unsuccessfully stifled a yawn.

"You've had a long day," Mrs. Allison said. "You mustn't let me just rattle on this way."

"I am tired. I think I'll take my bag to the bedroom and unpack. I can bring my bedding from the car later."

I left her listening to "Amos 'n' Andy." As I bent to lift my traveling case from the hall floor the chimes rang. I opened the door and looked down at a young boy standing on the porch.

"I have a letter," he said.

"I'll get Mrs. Allison." I glanced behind me, but she wasn't coming; she probably hadn't heard the bell.

"No, the letter's not for her. It's for Miss Medford."

"Oh? I'm Anne Medford."

He thrust an envelope into my hand, turned and ran down the porch steps. Back in the hall I tore a curl from the end of the envelope and tapped a single folded sheet of paper into my hand. The message was written in a large, scrawled script.

"I behaved very badly," I read. "Please forgive me." The note was signed "Jeremy Blackstock."

# Chapter 4

The next morning I woke to sunlight, a blue sky and birds chattering under the eaves. Steam knocked in the radiators beneath my windows with the promise of warmth to come. Karl's framed photograph smiled reassuringly from the nightstand: blond, thin-faced and handsome. He wore his brown sportcoat and the flowered tie, my present to him on his birthday. "To Anne, with all my love," he had written in his precise hand across a corner of the picture. I began to hum "Dream"—our song, Karl's and mine.

As I was dressing the strap on my slip broke. Still humming, I took the sewing kit out of my open traveling case. At the same time I unearthed another slip that I remembered was in need of mending.

The night before I had written to Karl, then uncovered and dusted the furniture in my bedroom. Now as I sewed I examined the room in daylight for the first time: an old-fashioned dresser with attached oval mirror, a chest of drawers, two straight chairs, an upholstered rocker, the arms of which ended in wooden knobs, and four long shelves of books. When I discovered books curiosity overcame my discretion. Mrs. Allison might peer from behind lace curtains—I loved to rummage through other people's libraries. However, I decided to save the pleasure till later.

All of the furniture was matched mahogany except the bed. The incongruity of the bed puzzled me—a metal bed whose gold paint had long since begun to peel and chip. The vertical bars on the head and foot were crowned by whorls and intricate curlicues.

"Oh!" Blood spotted my finger where I had jabbed myself with the needle. Annoyed, I licked the wound. When I finished sewing I put on my tan sweater and skirt. As I left the room I noticed a spring lock on the inside of the bedroom door. Odd, I thought. I brought my key ring from the dresser. One of the short, newer keys turned easily in the lock on the hall side of the door.

I returned the keys to the dresser. Why would someone put a spring lock on a bedroom door? When I was back in the hall I remembered the mismatched bed and looked in the other rooms for one made of mahogany. Without success. Had such a bed ever existed? I wondered.

When I came downstairs Mrs. Allison, her hair in curlers, was listening to Don McNeill's "Breakfast Club" while she dusted the living room. Two cats, one white, one black, lay curled asleep on a settee.

"Mail?" Mrs. Allison repeated in reply to my question. "We don't have home delivery in Canterbury. You'll have to pick your letters up at the window in the post office or rent a box there."

While she started the percolator I used her hall phone to call the telephone company. The white cat, MacArthur, rubbed against my legs until I lifted him into my lap. The girl who answered was polite but pessimistic. "No," she said, "I can't give you an installation date, Miss Medford, what with the war and all. Six or seven weeks, if you're lucky."

I called Quinlan's Service Station, told them I had a flat tire and, as Mrs. Allison had predicted, a young man appeared at our door shortly after. "Paul" I read from the patch on his shirt. He put on the spare and took the flat with him back to the garage. I felt better. I had begun to think I had wandered into a maze with all the turnings leading to dead ends.

The doorbell rang. A stout grey-haired man in a tan suit stood holding his broad-brimmed hat in his hand. He gave me a nod which stopped just short of being a bow.

"Miss Medford? Let me introduce myself. J. Powers Campbell. Is there a place where we can talk?" He looked over his head. "About your house."

Mrs. Allison had said I could use the parlor so I

invited him in. We sat on flowered chairs near the fire-place.

"I'll come right to the point, Miss Medford," he said in a loud, deep voice. "Ours is the largest, most successful real estate firm in the county. One of our clients is interested in your house. Have you given any thought to selling?"

"No, no I haven't. I've only just moved in."

"It's not often we get a buyer interested in one of these big old places. You're a very fortunate young woman. Did you have an asking price in mind?"

"No, I haven't really considered selling."

"My client is prepared to make a most generous offer. Most generous."

"Who is your client?" I wanted to know.

"I'm sorry," Mr. Campbell said. He took a handkerchief from his breast pocket and wiped his face. "I can't say at this stage of the negotiations—for business reasons. I'm sure you understand. I can tell you, though, we had in mind a figure in the neighborhood of forty thousand dollars."

I raised my eyebrows. My father had been made offers for the property, but never for anywhere near as much.

"You'll get cash money," Mr. Campbell said, "and we'll take care of all the paper work for you. I know women don't like to be bothered with details of that kind."

"You'll have to give me time to catch my breath," I said. "Can you call back? Perhaps next week?"

"Certainly. Take all the time you want." He leaned forward and lowered his voice. "To be honest," he said, "and just between us, I think my client's offer is generous in the extreme. I'd snap it up, little lady, if I were you."

When Mr. Campbell left I returned to the parlor surprised and delighted to think the house was worth so much. What would Father have done? I asked myself.

"Why is he willing to pay forty thousand dollars?" I could hear him ask. "Why won't he give his name?" I pondered the questions. Why? Was something of value concealed in the house or on the grounds? Anne Medford,

I thought, heiress. But where, I wondered, was my inheritance?

After coffee in the kitchen with Mrs. Allison I left her ironing while she listened to "John's Other Wife." I went upstairs determined to find drapes for my windows and, in the process, to seek clues to the unexplained value of the house. When a search of the second floor was unsuccessful I turned the key to open the attic door. Halfway to the top of the stairs something soft, like a wispy strand of a spiderweb, brushed my forehead, making me jerk back and grasp the rail to keep from falling. I looked up. A cord dangled in the stairwell. Annoyed with myself for being startled I pulled the cord and heard a click. Peering over my head to the shadowed ceiling I saw an empty light socket.

The attic was one huge room pierced by red brick chimneys—I counted six. The chimneys and posts supporting the roof created a feeling of incompleteness, as though this were the skeleton beginning of some vast architectural project. The area, probably because of the openness, seemed larger than the floor below, the whole greater than the sum of the parts.

From the peak, which must have been ten feet above my head, the roof sloped and angled to meet the attic floor. About a third of the way down I saw a rectangular trapdoor. Through the window at the top of the stairs I looked down over the bare branches of apple trees to a summerhouse above the river. Despite a similar window on the far wall and other small oval and circular windows in the gables—some with stained glass panes—the room was so large it remained shrouded in perpetual twilight. This attic, like the rest of the house, seemed alien to me. I felt like an intruder.

I searched for draperies among hoardings of a stranger's yesterdays—in the drawers of discarded furniture, amidst a maze of boxes, wardrobes and piles of old copies of *Reader's Digest, Better Homes and Gardens* and *The Ladies' Home Journal*. In vain. Hopefully I lifted the lid of a trunk only to find stacked newspapers,

the somber headlines on the top paper proclaiming
LINDBERG BABY FOUND DEAD.

Discouraged, I returned to my room where I debated
whether to wear a coat, decided not to and went downstairs to my car. I looked back at the stark grey house.
To somebody, I thought, you're worth forty thousand
dollars. When I glanced next door I saw a black Cadillac parked in the Blackstock driveway, but no sign of either Jeremy or his father.

At the post office the counter windows were closed.
After I mailed my letter to Karl I approached one of
the women waiting in the lobby. "This can't be a holiday,"
I said.

"They're sorting the mail from the ten o'clock train,"
she told me. "Should be about done." She was right.
In a few minutes the windows rumbled open and I took
my place in line.

"Anne Medford." The postmaster, a slight, sandy-
haired man, repeated my name, then removed letters
from the "M" slot behind him and shuffled through them.
"Sorry, nothing today," he said. I felt a twinge of disappointment. It's too soon to expect his letter, I told myself.
I rented a box and the postmaster wrote the combination
for me on a slip of paper.

I drove to Quinlan's. Inside I found the young man,
Paul, who had changed my tire bent over the engine
of a sedan. I stood by the door feeling unsure of myself,
as I always did in garages. When he saw me, Paul
straightened and wiped his hands on a dirty rag.

He rolled a mounted tire across the cement floor and
stopped in front of me with the wheel between us. "I
went over your tire and tube real good," Paul said, shaking his head. "I couldn't find anything wrong, no nail or
nothing. Seems O.K. to me." He bounced the tire a
few times on the floor. "Want me to put it on for your
spare?"

I nodded. "The tire was flat, wasn't it?" I asked him.

"Yeah, no question about that. Flat as a pancake."
He bolted the spare in the trunk of my Dodge. "Kids
celebrating Halloween early most likely," he said.

"Funny, though. Not many kids in your part of town. Hardly any at all."

I was puzzled. Children I had known didn't let air out of tires. For an instant I wondered if, since I was a teacher, the act had been deliberate, malicious and aimed at me, Anne Medford. No, unlikely, I thought.

After I thanked and paid the mechanic I walked past the honor roll to the variety store to look for make-do drapes. I found what I wanted on a shelf next to the blackout curtains, but when I got them home they were too short and I had to go back for a longer set. I spent the rest of the day hanging drapes, shopping and cleaning.

I lay in bed that night staring at the moonlight coming through the slit where one set of drapes didn't quite meet. I twisted this way and that. The door creaked open. I got up, but the door refused to click shut so I pushed the small knob and the lock sprang into place. This must be the reason for the lock, I decided. I turned the doorhandle and pushed. Good, I thought, the door won't budge. The last I remembered was listening to a distant church bell toll midnight.

The next day, Friday, I wore my tartan skirt and a green jacket when I walked to the afternoon faculty orientation. I was excited, for this was my first day on my first real job. Although I was five minutes early I was the last to arrive, so I sat near the back of the third-floor study hall where the meeting was being held.

There were five rows of desks in the room, all bolted to the floor, each with a seat folding down from the desk behind. The tops, scarred with initials and names, had pencil slots at the top and round ink-bottle holes in the upper-right-hand corners. There were no ink bottles. I felt I had gone back to my own high school days and wondered if four years had been enough to change me from student into teacher.

My seat was comfortable, but I noticed the three men in the group had to put their legs in the aisles. Two of them were older, in their fifties, I guessed. The other, though, was a big pleasant-looking young man who smiled when he saw me glance at him. I returned his smile and quickly turned away, embarrassed.

"We're going to have a wonderful year in 1944–45," Mr. Burke, the principal, told us. He walked back and forth at the front of the room pushing a strand of white hair from his eyes. He reminded me of Mr. Chips. Probably his wife had died tragically and now Mr. Burke, beloved by his students, made Canterbury High School his whole life.

"All of us have to work together," he went on, "to create a meaningful and enriching curriculum, to prepare Canterbury students to take their places in the world. This year we've been asked to emphasize mathematics and, for the first time, we're offering a full four years of math: algebra, trigonometry, plane and solid geometry and a special class in the slide rule."

I smiled to myself. Math was being singled out and I was the teacher. Mr. Burke was depending on me—I vowed to do the best I could.

"We also plan to begin a mathematics club," Mr. Burke went on, "with the help of our new math teacher, Miss Medford. Stand up, Miss Medford, stand up." I did, blushing.

"Let me introduce the other new teachers," Mr. Burke said. He consulted a card in his hand. I tried to associate names with faces. I'm not good at names. One reason might be a habit I have of identifying people I don't know with movie stars they resemble. Among the fifteen women on the Canterbury High School faculty I found a June Allyson, a Hedy Lamarr and a Merle Oberon. Most of the others were Spring Byingtons. There was one Marjorie Main. When the returning teachers introduced themselves I learned the young man's name was Don Nevins.

Mr. Burke handed out schedules for the school year and our homeroom assignments. "The first meeting of the PTA is a week from Thursday night," he said. "The parents are putting on their annual reception for the teachers so I hope we'll have the usual one hundred percent faculty turnout."

When the meeting ended most of the other teachers stopped to tell me they hoped I'd like the school and Canterbury. I was one of the last to leave.

"The same old crap." Don Nevins caught up with me as I walked down the wide staircase.

"I thought the meeting was interesting," I said. "Of course, it's my first."

"Talk, talk, talk. All they do is talk." He held the heavy main door for me. Even though he wore a heavy glen-plaid jacket I could see he was broad shouldered. His hair was blond with a gentle wave. Van Johnson, I decided. "How about a cup of coffee?" he asked.

"I'd like one."

"Santoro's is the only place with good coffee. It's over by the five corners. You teach math, don't you? This is a mathematics year, I can see that already. Last year aviation. P.E. the year before, after so many men flunked their army physicals. After the war we'll have a Russian year and a French year and a Spanish year. Wendell Willkie, one world, and so forth."

"And what do you teach?"

"English. Prose and poetry grades seven through twelve. We've never had an English year. Probably never will. I'm sorry. I must sound awfully cynical. We've really got some great teachers, and great students, too. You have one senior who must be almost a math genius, Carroll Johnson. He's a Negro." As we entered the restaurant I glanced at the war news on the front page of the papers in the rack.

"But this town is as dead as the proverbial doornail," Don said after we sat at a table. "The only reason I stay," he lowered his voice, "is because I'm writing a novel—a satirical novel about the so-called teaching profession and about schools of education."

"That's wonderful," I said. I was impressed.

"I've been writing the book off and on for the last four years," he said. "I started when I worked summers

at the World's Fair to pay my way through college.
I've written more than a hundred pages. You may think
I'm slow, but I want it to be right."

"I'd like to read your book when it's finished."

"You will. Of course, I can't let the people at the
school see it while I'm still teaching here because I use
some of them as characters." Don put cream and sugar
in his coffee and stirred. His eyes, I noticed, were the
color of the coffee. I smiled at him, for how often was I
chosen in preference to June Allyson, Hedy Lamarr
and Merle Oberon?

He walked home with me along shaded streets beneath
September trees of yellow, orange and gold. An old
man stood on the curb in front of the library, rake in
hand, staring into the flames from a pile of burning
leaves. I breathed deeply. This was a day, I thought,
for football games and marching bands and chrysanthemum corsages.

"Oh, you live next door to the Blackstocks," Don
said when we reached the white fence. Their yard was
deserted, the tight row of pines impassive. "I didn't
teach here then, of course," Don said, "but the son,
Jeremy, is a legend at the high school."

"How do you mean a legend?"

"In sports. Soccer, basketball, baseball, tennis. Say,
do you play?"

"Tennis? Yes, a little."

"Swell! We'll have to get together for a few sets. There
are only the two courts so we'll have to go early."

"I'd love to. You were saying about Jeremy Blackstock?"

"Yes, he was one of those natural athletes who comes
along once every five years or so. Had a terrible temper,
though, and got thrown out of a couple of basketball
games for fighting. The school won three county cham-
pionships his senior year. They never won that many
before or since. We don't play football here in Canterbury—soccer instead. Football, that's how I got my trick
knee, playing guard for Union." I must have looked
blank. "A small college upstate," he explained.

"A funny thing about Jeremy Blackstock, though," Don said.

"What is?"

"I never realized until last year that he lived here in the village. When people talk about him it's always in the past tense, as if he were dead."

Don left me at the porch steps. "It was good getting to know you," he said. I watched him stroll down the drive whistling "Mairzy Doats." He turned when he reached the road and waved and I smiled and waved back.

Feeling more alive than I had for days I went upstairs to start supper. My mood lasted through an evening of listening to music on the radio and preparing lesson plans.

I was surprised when I couldn't sleep. My hand throbbed; I turned on the light and put salve on the sore where I had pricked my finger with the needle. When at last sleep came I was troubled by dreams, but on waking in the morning I could not recall them—could only remember seeing phantom shapes and hearing muffled voices.

The door creaked. I put on my robe and walked across the room. The lock was drawn back, letting the door swing free. I had locked the door, hadn't I? I let the door stand open while I looked about the room and in the closet. Nothing, nothing at all.

If the door had been locked before I went to bed, and I was sure it had been, then who had come in the night to unlock it? And how? And for what reason? Despite the heat hissing from the radiators I felt cold and, shivering, folding my arms across my chest. There was a wrongness about this room, this house, that I didn't understand. Without warning I knew the chill beginnings of fear.

# Chapter 5

I convinced myself I had forgotten to lock the bedroom door. No other explanation was possible—there were only two keys; I had brought one with me and Mrs. Allison had returned the other the day before. I had simply failed to lock the door.

I couldn't decide what to wear; I finally settled on a brown skirt and sweater outfit I had often worn at college. I felt tense and nervous, was impatient with Mrs. Allison and found myself wishing this were Monday instead of an aimless Saturday. Even the letter waiting at the post office failed to change my mood. I scanned Karl's backhanded script for his personal comments before reading the letter through word by word.

Karl, a training officer at Camp Blanding, wrote that a new group of draftees had arrived from Fort Dix and one of the men, an eighteen-year-old boy actually, had tried to hang himself in the shower. I shivered. Why would anyone, no matter how depressed or distraught, try to take his own life? If today disappointed you, tomorrow would be better.

Around noon, as I worked on lesson plans, the Cadillac pulled from the driveway next door. The Blackstock house seemed deserted. In the afternoon I walked under grey skies along quiet village streets and later explored the rest of the house. I seemed immobile, frozen, unable to begin anything new.

Back in my bedroom I knelt in front of the bookcase. I nodded when I saw the familiar titles: *Anthony Adverse, Gone with the Wind, Oil for the Lamps of China, Arrowsmith*, the complete works of Dickens still in their transparent jackets.

Then I found four books at the end of the bottom shelf. I blushed at the photographs of men and women performing strange and grotesque acts. My face burning,

I returned the books to the shelf. Whose were they? What should I do with them?

Late in the afternoon, restless, feeling closed in, I went outside and followed a path beside the remains of what must have been Mrs. Allison's victory garden. Beyond the garden I walked among the apple trees where flies buzzed around rotted fruit on the ground while over my head branches laced together in geometric patterns. The path ended at the summerhouse, an open building with a frame of cedar limbs supporting a cone-shaped roof.

When I entered spiders scurried into crevices in the floor. I looked down to the river and saw shadows reach like fingers from the near shore out over the water. A haze obscured the far bank. I heard a boat purr on the river, a dog bark, the happy cries of children in the distance. My throat tightened and I felt empty, desolate.

I remembered another autumn evening years before, sailing through the channel and around the point as we hurried to reach home before dark, my hair streaming behind, Father, at the tiller, pointing to our house waiting for us at the edge of the pines.

I felt a longing for him stronger, more palpable, than any I had felt before. Help me, I wanted to cry out. Father, I need you, the reassurance of your optimism, the shelter of your concern. Suddenly I sobbed—long, deep, wrenching sobs. Stop, I told myself. I dug my fingernails into the palms of my hands. I was shaking, frightened by my loss of control.

I slowly climbed the hill back toward the dark and somber house. I should have been ready, but I was not. The Blackstock dog ran snarling along the far side of the fence, making me flinch. The Doberman loped beside the barrier, stopping to probe for an opening. Finding none, he growled deep in his throat. Even as I walked quickly away I looked over my shoulder to the Blackstock house, half expecting . . . what? Jeremy to stride toward me as he had on the day of my arrival?

I was almost to the orchard when I saw MacArthur

scuttle across the lawn. He leaped to the top of the porch steps and onto the railing; then he grasped the post with all four legs and clawed his way to the top, where he clung beneath the overhang.

I tensed. Suddenly the Blackstock Doberman ran around the corner of the house, *my* house, leaped to the porch, and thrust his front paws on the rail. His jaws strained toward the cat. How had he escaped from his yard? Standing as still as I could, I waited. Don't move, I told myself. The house was about two hundred feet away. If you don't move, he won't see you. I bit my lip. Once more I looked to the Blackstock yard; I saw neither Jeremy nor his father. No car was in the driveway. No lights glowed in the dusk.

The sun was down. Could dogs see in the dark? In the sky long streamers of clouds, orange a few minutes before, changed to pink, then grew black. On the porch the cat, claws sunk into the wood of the post, inched higher until I could see only his tail from under the eaves.

Brutus dropped to the porch floor and stalked back and forth, stopping occasionally to look up at the cat. I glanced around me, not moving, and saw the orchard twenty feet to my left. Halfway to the trees a dark mound showed where leaves and brush had been piled long ago.

Grudgingly, Brutus lifted his siege. He was poised at the top of the steps, nose high, reconnoitering. I held my breath; I could hear my heart pounding. The dog trotted down the stairs, paused at the bottom, then turned to walk along the path in the direction of the fence. I sighed. He hadn't seen me. Don't stop, I told him under my breath, keep going, just a few more feet. A few more feet and I would be hidden from him by the forsythias at the corner of the house.

Two birds flitted in front of Brutus, swooped low toward me, their wings a blur, and whirred over my head toward a tree at the edge of the yard. The dog stopped, curious; he seemed to follow the flight of the birds and stood almost in the point of a hunting dog.

I drew in my breath, held steady, afraid to breathe as the dog took a few tentative steps in my direction, then paused once more. I clenched my hands at my sides. Please God, I thought, don't let him see me.

From the river behind me I heard the whistle of a ship and the cry of gulls. The scene, for an instant, was a still life: my house with the blank stares of the windows and the chimneys and peaks dark against the sky, the Blackstock house silent and squat, the orchard's intertwining limbs reaching high above my head. All this I seemed to know rather than see, for all my senses were concentrated on the dog.

Brutus moved ahead, his nose down. A scream caught in my throat. He'd found me. For a few seconds he stopped, tensed, then lunged forward. My legs tightened with fear and I was unable to move.

The dog loped over the grass in long fluid strides. He was halfway to me, making no sound, intent. All at once I could move. I turned and ran to my left toward the mound of brush. I stumbled on a clump of grass, almost fell, recovered and darted to the far side of the pile, reaching into the tangle. I could hear the dog's feet on the dry grass. I tugged at branches, threw aside sodden leaves. My hand closed on a limb. I pulled and the limb moved, then caught. I yanked sideways and felt the stick swing in my hand; yet it refused to come loose. I pulled in desperation. The stick jerked free from the pile and I almost fell backwards to the ground. I steadied myself. In my hand I held a cut branch more than three feet long and as thick as my wrist.

Brutus stopped some twenty feet away and stared at me and the weapon in my hand. He crouched. A lean muscular animal, brown and black, he seemed to coil himself; then he sprang forward and as he leaped all I could see was his white teeth coming at my throat.

I held the stick in both hands straight toward him, afraid to use it like a club for fear he would be on me while I swung. His chest struck the jagged end. The force of his hurtling body jolted my arms and I stepped back, stunned.

The dog yelped, a cry of surprise and pain. He fell to the ground and I felt a surge of hope as he staggered, gagging, but he kept on his feet and with a snarl charged again, low to the ground. I warded him off with the stick, prodded him as I backed away. He seized the end of the stick in his teeth and twisted his head from side to side. The rough bark stung my hands as I fought to keep my hold.

I jabbed at him while turning to keep him in front of me, afraid he would elude the stick and reach me with his teeth before I could protect myself. The dog, the wood still clenched between his jaws, snarled and stiffened his front legs as he pulled at the stick. My hands stung; my breath came in quick, shallow gasps. In a moment I would lose my hold and the Doberman would be on me, ripping and tearing.

The apple trees. I glanced over my head and had the impression of limbs above and behind. I had walked beneath the trees only a half hour before and now I tried to picture them in my mind. Good-sized trees, I remembered, twenty feet or more in height. Could I climb into the lower branches or were they too high? Close to the ground, I thought; but I could not be sure.

With a last effort I lifted my end of the stick and hurled it from me with all my strength. The dog spun away, the branch in his mouth, and I turned and ran. Behind me I heard Brutus snarl and in my mind I pictured him abandoning the stick to lunge at me.

The lowest limb of the nearest tree branched only a few feet off the ground. As my hand touched the grey trunk I stepped on a rotten apple, slipped to one side and staggered but did not fall. I scrambled to the lowest limb while I reached over my head for a new handhold.

I heard the dog's feet scatter leaves under the tree. As I pulled myself up I felt a searing pain as my knee scraped a protruding limb. With both feet on a branch, I reached higher. The branch sagged under me and I heard the ominous crack of splitting wood. I grasped a higher limb and pulled myself up just as Brutus caught my shoe with his fangs.

I hung suspended, the dog's whole weight pulling me down, the branch bending in my hands. I twisted my body, but still the dog clung to my foot. I twisted again and felt his grip loosen; he fell away. With the toe of one foot against the trunk I reached with the other to a higher branch. I climbed until I slumped onto a firm limb high above the ground. With my arms about the trunk I leaned my head on the tree, gasping for breath.

The dog stood on his hind legs with his front paws on the tree, then dropped to the ground. He barked once, twice, and was gone into the darkness. I sat trembling. Did the dog lurk out there in the night?

After what seemed an eternity headlights swooped along the Blackstock drive. Their porch light came on and I saw Brutus jump playfully to greet the two men. I climbed from the tree and ran to my house. Inside I lay on the bed, arms sore, my knee stinging. I shut my eyes. When at last I was calmer I called the Blackstocks. Charles answered.

"Brutus?" he said, surprise in his voice. "You surely must be mistaken. There's no possible way for Brutus to get out of the yard. The dog didn't hurt you, did it?"

"No, but I'm not mistaken. He attacked me."

"He was here locked in when we came home." Mr. Blackstock hesitated as though considering other possibilities. "There are lots of dogs in the neighborhood," he said. "One of them, perhaps?"

"No, I'm sure it was your dog." I sounded more positive than I felt. He seemed so certain. Could I really be sure?

"I don't know what to say. You're welcome to look at our fences and gates. Brutus could only get away if someone opened a gate, and no one would be foolish enough to do that."

I was still angry when I hung up. I was positive Brutus was the dog that had attacked me. If he couldn't get out of the Blackstock yard by himself, he had been let out. From the tone of his voice I could tell Charles

Blackstock doubted my story. Did he think me nothing but an hysterical girl?

When I returned to my room I examined the jagged teeth marks on the heels of my shoe. There was nothing imaginary about them. The moon was rising over the mountains and its light reflected off the river below me. The branches of the trees in the apple orchard seemed to be twisted in grotesque patterns. Far away, a dog barked. I undressed and slid between the covers, but I knew sleep would be long in coming.

# Chapter 6

I spent Sunday afternoon trying to get interested in a novel. In the evening I listened to the radio and, though the regular shows were back for the winter season, neither Jack Benny nor Fred Allen brought me from my lethargy. I felt as dreary as the day itself had been. The smell of rain was in the air, clouds obscured the summits of the mountains, the river flowed grey and sluggish—yet no rain fell. That night I twisted and turned in bed for what seemed hours before I slept. I couldn't understand my insomnia, for usually I went to sleep at once.

School began on Monday. I was excited and nervous, edgy because of my lack of sleep, but from the time I wrote "Miss Anne Medford" on the blackboard to begin my algebra class the week went well—with one exception.

The students were alert and appeared interested. When Mr. Burke stopped by just before the final bell on the second day of school he was smiling.

"They like you," he told me, nodding at the boys and girls leaving the room carrying their two-ring binders and textbooks.

"Well," I said, "I like them."

"Just stop in the office and let me know if you ever

need anything. We try to give our new teachers all the help we can."

On Tuesday Don waved to me in the hall and the next day he winked at me outside the teachers' lounge. "Remember the tennis," he said.

"Why don't we decide on a day?" I asked.

"Oh," he said, as though the idea hadn't occurred to him before. "Yes, let's. I'll give you a call."

My failure came on Thursday. I sat at my desk after school checking homework papers, my eyes going first to the clock on the rear wall, then to the door. This was the day of the first meeting of the math club. Carroll Johnson, a dark Negro with tight-curled black hair, came into the room, dropped two books on a desk in the front row and sat whistling soundlessly to himself. Two other boys looked in from the corridor. I smiled and they nodded, walked in and sat behind Carroll. The clock moved ahead, minute by minute. Would no one else come? How long should I wait?

I gave up after ten minutes. The math club would have to start with only three members. I told them we would explore college-level concepts, play math games and experiment with puzzles. I tried not to show my disappointment with the turnout, but I don't know how successful I was. If I didn't find a way to arouse more interest I knew we would have to disband.

"You didn't go out for soccer?" I asked Carroll when he stayed after the meeting to show me a slide rule he was making.

"No, Miss Medford," he said.

"Do you play basketball or baseball?" He was a tall, well-developed boy.

"No, m'am," he said. "I don't seem to be able to get interested in sports."

"Oh," I said, surprised. From all appearances he would make a good athelete. At any rate, from what I had seen of Carroll so far I knew he would be a better math student than any I had known when I was a student or when I was practice teaching.

After I answered his questions about the slide rule

he left and I sat in the deserted classroom with my hands clasped on my desk. Did Carroll's being a Negro cause the other students to stay away from the club? I hoped not, but I wondered.

That evening, at home, the phone rang in the down-stairs hall. "For you," Mrs. Allison called up the stairs.

"Powers Campbell," the booming voice said.

I had thought about the offer to buy the house. Despite Brutus, despite my uneasiness, I didn't want to move, knowing how difficult finding an apartment would be. I saw the house as a challenge I must meet and overcome. Besides, I told myself, this is one of the few tangible reminders I have of my father and, in a way, of my mother, too.

"I'm sorry," I told Mr. Campbell. "I just don't want to consider selling now."

"What if my client raised his offer? I don't know that he will, you understand, but would you recon-sider?"

"No, I want to see how things go for awhile. My mind's made up."

"I'll keep in touch," Mr. Campbell promised.

After school on Friday, I found a letter from Karl in my mailbox. I put my books on the post-office writing stand and tore open the envelope. "Weather's still hot," Karl wrote. "Killed a snake on the rifle range yesterday . . . fifteen-mile march tomorrow with full packs . . . the new captain is a regular General Patton, swagger stick and all." For three pages Karl reported the news from Camp Blanding. Then, in the last two paragraphs: "I remember the good times we had last winter . . . skating at the lake . . . the way you looked when the sled turned over. . . . I miss you, think about you." He signed the letter, as he always did, "Love, Karl."

Disappointed, I returned the letter to the envelope. I sensed a coldness—no, not a coldness—a lack of warmth. The two are different. I felt hurt, even angry, but not surprised.

I walked with fallen leaves rustling beneath my feet. Children ran past calling to one another, the pitch of their voices celebrating freedom from the first week of school. I was tired, discouraged by the house, worried about the math club, faced with the emptiness of another weekend. For a moment I allowed myself the escape, the bittersweet pleasure, of self-pity.

Yet the fault was mine. Karl had every right to withdraw, every reason. And he was withdrawing, not consciously, perhaps, but inexorably all the same. And not to wound me, but to protect himself. Could I really tell this from two paragraphs of a letter written in haste? I should have laughed at my foolishness, but I did not—for I knew I was right.

The longer Karl and I were separated the more difficult it became for me to reach out to him. And the initiative had to be mine, not his. Soon I wouldn't be able to say, "No, don't go. Forget the evening at the lake. Let's give ourselves another chance."

Why couldn't I be warm and loving like other women? I could not—even if given a second chance I would act as I had acted last summer—or worse. I wanted to cry out against the unfairness, but since my father's death there was no one to listen.

I clenched my hands in the pockets of my jacket. The fault was not my father's. He had done the best he could and I had received more affection, more love, than most girls with *two* parents—or so I thought. I was the way I was. Why, I did not know. I only knew I had pushed the memory of that summer night far into the recesses of my mind. I went for days without remembering—but then a word, a man's sudden laugh, the splash of water would bring back the raft, the bed in the moonlight and Karl.

Was something the matter with me? Was I ill? No, I told myself. My father had died only six weeks before. I was upset, distraught. At another time, with a different man . . .

I knew I deceived myself. I admired people who faced the truth, however unpleasant. Face the truth, Anne, I told myself, face the truth.

Karl had come home on a three-day pass. On our last night together he took me to a movie, *Waterloo Bridge,* and we sat near the rear of the theater, our fingers interlaced on my lap. Since Karl's proposal and my hesitation we had been trying to reestablish our comfortable "going-together" relationship of the winter before.

As I watched the movie—a romance set in England during the first World War—I was distracted by Karl's hand on mine. I felt I needed him, needed someone to care. In the film's final scene Robert Taylor, a grey-haired Army officer, leaned on the rail of Waterloo Bridge and stared down at the water as he mourned the girl he had loved and lost years before. Tears came to my eyes and I dabbed at my face with a handkerchief as we left the theater.

On the sidewalk outside, Karl returned the salute of two enlisted men and I was proud of him, proud to be with him. "Would you like to go dancing?" Karl asked.

"I don't know if I should," I said, thinking of my father. Karl nodded, solicitous as always. At times I wished he would pay less attention to what I wanted. Or did I really mean less attention to what I *said* I wanted?

"Let's drive to the lake," I suggested. "It's so hot and muggy in town." I still had the key to the lake house, although the lawyers planned to auction the furnishings and put the house itself up for sale to help settle father's debts.

"I can't afford the place," Father had told me, "but on the other hand I've always wanted a house on a lake where I could own a sailboat." The house, when he'd bought it, had been old and in need of paint. I must have showed my dismay when I saw it for the first time. "Don't worry," my father had said, "we'll soon have her shipshape." And we did. I came to love the lake and the days we spent there, my father and I.

At the lake, Karl stopped the car at the hotel first.

"Wait," he said as we entered the lobby with its huge fieldstone fireplace, "I want to hear this." The radio behind the front desk was playing loudly. "American armored columns," the announcer said, "continue their drive to turn the German flank in Normandy. . . ." The invasion had begun a few weeks before.

"I hope you don't have to go overseas," I said.

"Sometimes I hope the same. I get scared thinking about how I'll handle myself—can't imagine killing someone. Yet other times I want to go, want to be a part of the war. To me it's almost like a crusade."

We paused in the doorway to the lounge. The summer season had begun and, despite the war, the room was full, mostly couples, servicemen and their girls. I sipped a Manhattan, a drink my father had taught me to like, while we talked.

"Want to try my drink?" I asked.

Karl shook his head. He was drinking beer.

"Here," I said, removing the cherry, which was speared on a toothpick, "try this anyway." Karl rolled the cherry in his mouth before eating it. He made a face.

"No, not for me," he said.

I laughed at him. We were at ease with one another and, wanting to make the moment last, I nodded when he asked if I'd like another drink. Karl walked to the jukebox, gaudily lighted in reds, greens and yellows. "This nickel's for you," he said as he put the coin in the slot. I pushed the button for "Harbor Lights."

As I listened to the music, the shuffle of dancers' feet and the murmur of voices, I leaned my head on the back of the booth, enjoying the warmth spreading through me. Other girls glanced appraisingly at Karl, handsome in his uniform, but when I looked across the booth his eyes were on me. I felt pretty and desirable.

"We'd better go," Karl said, "if we're going to get to your father's place."

"Ummm," I said, reaching for his hand after I slid from the booth. When we crossed the parking lot to the car I leaned on him and his lips brushed my hair.

We parked in the driveway of the lake house and

walked down the gravel road to the dock my father
had built. Reflections from lights on the far shore rippled
on the water and waves lapped against the pilings. Was
this a mistake, I wondered, coming here? This lake
and this house had so many memories.

"Come on," I said, as my throat tightened, "let's
go swimming. We've got suits in the house." I ran ahead
of him along the drive to the porch and unlocked the
door. While Karl waited in the living room I rummaged
through drawers until I found the bathing suits. "Here."
I handed him a pair of blue trunks. "You can change
in the downstairs bathroom." He was familiar with the
house, for he had visited many times when my father
was alive.

In my bedroom on the second floor I pulled on my
one-piece suit. It was white with a short flared skirt.
I looked for a cap but couldn't find one.

Karl was waiting on the porch and we walked across
the lawn hand in hand. I dived from the dock, swam
underwater until my lungs hurt, then surfaced, gasping
from the shock of the cold water. Karl swam beside
me to the raft where he swung up, reached for my hand
and pulled me up beside him. We staggered, off balance,
and his arm came around me and we kissed, his body
wet, his lips cool, his tongue unexpected on mine. I was
excited, dizzy, yet at the same time I felt a surge
of panic. I put my hands on his chest and moved back
a step.

We lay side by side on the raft, hands clasped, legs
lightly touching, listening to the water and the sound
of laughter from the hotel. I sat up and folded my arms
on my knees; my hair was wet and cold on my neck.
Karl turned onto one elbow, watching me.

"Your last night," I said. I looked over the water
at the dark jagged outline of the pine trees against the
sky.

"I may get a leave this fall," he said, "but everything's
up in the air since the invasion started." I turned from
him and stared over the side of the raft into the black
depths of the water. Tonight, I thought, might be the

last time I'll see him for months or years or even, and I shivered with foreboding, or even forever. Each moment seemed underscored with urgency, a sense of the passing of the few hours we had together.

The lake, the beach, and the trees glowed in the moonlight. On impulse I leaned to Karl and kissed him on the lips, but when he reached for me I ran to the edge of the raft and dived. I heard him plunge in after me and we raced toward shore.

I got there first and ran across the dock, laughing, Karl just behind. He caught me on the lawn, swung me around, put his leg in back of mine and gently pushed me to the ground. All at once we stopped laughing. I looked at him standing over me with water glistening on his body. He seemed so young without his uniform.

We walked back to the house, not talking, hands apart, not touching. Once his fingers brushed my side and I trembled.

I squeezed his hand when I left him in front of the dark fireplace. Upstairs in the bathroom I unzipped and peeled off my suit. After I dried myself I wrapped the towel around my body and opened the bathroom door. Suddenly timid, I clutched the towel tightly over my breasts before I tiptoed through the empty hall to my room. My clothes lay on the chair. I opened the closet, let the towel drop to the floor, pulled on an old pongee dressing gown and tied the sash about my waist.

I rolled up the shade and the moonlight fell across the bed. I lay on my back with hands at my sides, the gown smooth on my skin. The stair creaked. My breathing was shallow and rapid. Outside a car swished past on the road. I sensed a movement and I knew Karl was standing in the doorway. I stared at the shadowed ceiling, my body stiff and straight. Karl walked to the bed and looked down at me. I could hear his breathing.

"Anne," he whispered, his voice husky. I made no move. I must give him no sign, I thought. He lay on his side next to me. His hand touched my wet hair, caressed my face and neck, moved down the front of my gown to the sash. I felt a pull and the sash drew tight, then parted. When Karl's hand touched my waist my skin seemed to shrink away of its own accord.

He ran his fingers over my bare hip to my legs, the gown sliding apart. I tensed and closed my eyes. I felt the mere whisper of his touch on the inside of my leg. I stiffened and his hand left me. He edged closer, not touching, yet so close I could feel his body next to mine.

"Anne," he said, "I want you so much." I murmured, making sounds, not words. His hand returned, more forceful now, and he pulled me onto my side and held me to him. He was warm and his body was lean and hard.

I saw the steel tips of the umbrellas. Black huddled umbrellas. Umbrellas slick with rain. Nausea rose in me, revulsion, and I knew I had to get away, escape. I rolled from him onto my back. His hand gripped my wrist.

"No, I can't," I whispered urgently. I jerked my hand free and ran from the room.

"Anne, Anne!" he called after me. I leaned against the inside of the closed bathroom door, sobbing, sick and ashamed. I heard him in the hall repeating my name and, though I couldn't be sure, I thought he was crying.

Later, after I dressed and combed my hair, I found Karl sitting in the car. Neither that night nor the next morning when I kissed him good-bye as he boarded the bus for camp, nor in any of our letters, did we mention or even allude to what had happened at the lake.

But I knew he would not forget. Nor would I. Ever.

# Chapter 7

I awakened on Saturday morning to find nothing changed: my bedroom door was locked as it had been each morning all week, the promise of tennis with Don Nevins remained only a promise and I had heard nothing

from Jeremy Blackstock since his note on the evening
of my arrival in Canterbury.

For the last week I had expected Jeremy to follow
his note with a visit or a phone call. Now I suspected
he had realized the obtuseness of his behavior, had written
the note to balance his ledgers and considered the matter
closed.

What are you going to do? I asked myself. Do you
plan to pine away imprisoned in your castle until a prince
rides forth to rescue you? I faced a shortage of princes.
Don Nevins? I smiled. He seemed an unlikely savior.
You have to rescue yourself, I thought. My father may
have been a dreamer, but he worked hard to make his
dreams come true.

I pushed the drapes aside and looked down on a
lawn white with frost. Next door the Doberman was
nowhere to be seen. I stepped into brown slacks and
pulled a red-and-white ski sweater over my head. When
I brushed my hair I grimaced at the combination of
colors. No matter, I thought, I'd be warm for the work
I had to do. I was eager to begin.

After orange juice, toast and coffee I went downstairs
to find Mrs. Allison in an excited dither. "Friday," she
told me, "the major is coming from Boston. Next Friday,
for the weekend. He's going to drive me to Long Island
to see my sister." She lifted knickknacks to dust beneath
them. "You must have dinner with us Friday night.
We won't leave till Saturday morning. I do so want
you to meet my son."

"Yes, I'd like to," I said. Mrs. Allison nodded when
I asked to use her phone.

I looked in the telephone book for Johnson. What
was his father's name? Yes, there—Frank.

"Number please," the operator said.

"385–P," I told her. I heard the ring and a young
girl's voice answered. He probably has a large family,
I thought. "Carroll Johnson?" I asked. In a few minutes
the boy came on the line.

"Carroll? This is Miss Medford. I wondered if you'd

be interested in doing yard work for me?" I sensed
a hesitation.

"Yes, I would, if you have a job that really needs
doing," he said at last. Why would he think I'd offer
him busy work? I wondered.

"Fine," I said. "I'll pay you fifty cents an hour. All
right? When can you start? The sooner the better."

"Would this afternoon be too soon?"

"Wonderful. Do you know where I live? Eleven Spruce
Street, in the big house."

I hung up feeling pleased. I was sure Carroll could
use the money as much as I needed his help. I walked
back upstairs to my bedroom. I'll start here, I thought.
Three walls and most of the fourth were papered with
faded red roses twining on trellises. Behind my bed
a short section of the wall was paneled with wood
as though, when it was almost finished, the builder had
sought to give the room variety. Should I paper the
wood too?

I examined the walls more closely. The paper was
yellowed and had begun to peel at the edges. I'd do
the papering myself, I decided. When I'd helped my
father fix one of our homes to sell before we moved
to another town and another business, I had learned
to hang wallpaper and, though I still had a thousand
dollars in the bank from the sale of father's car, I would
need all that money and more.

I had noticed a tool chest in the cellar, so I descended
to the underground room. I was in luck—a builder's tape
measure lay in a jumble of T squares, nails, screws,
pliers and saws. This will be a good day, I thought.

Armed with a pen, a notebook and the tape, I went
outside and around to the back of the house. The white
cat followed. He walked with distaste into the wet grass
and then scurried to the porch, where he lay on the
railing in the sun. The air was brisk with intimations
of the winter to come. The sweater felt rough on my
bare arms and I remembered skating parties, building
snowmen in front of the dormitory, drinking hot chocolate
by the fire. I liked winter.

I placed the tape on the ground, fastened the metal loop with a stick and unrolled the tape. I marked the spot with a stone, pushed the button on the side of the leather holder and the tape snapped back.

"May I help?" I jumped. An older man stood by the porch steps. Smiling, he walked toward me. I recognized him as the man I had seen shoveling coal in the cellar.

"I'm Charles Blackstock," he said. "I'm sorry if I startled you. We talked on the phone last weekend."

"I'm Anne Medford." He bowed. He was a tall, husky man with white hair flowing to his collar in back. His face was thin with a long nose—a stern face except when he smiled. He reminded me of the pictures in history books of Andrew Jackson.

"About the dog," he said. "The more I've thought about it the surer I am Brutus wasn't involved." I didn't reply.

"I apologize for not calling on you sooner," he went on, "but we've been away, my son and I." He looked at the tape in my hand. "I see you're measuring."

"Oh," I said, my voice stiff. "Yes, I'm thinking of making some improvements in the house. Just the yard and my bedroom for now." I lifted my head to indicate the window of my room. "Today I'm getting down the outside dimensions of the house."

Charles Blackstock glanced up at the dead ivy clinging to the weathered wood on the side of the house and shook his head. "Sending good money after bad, in my opinion."

"But it's a beautiful old house," I protested. I was surprised by my reaction—after all, he was probably right. "Look at the gables," I went on, "and the chimneys and the view up the river. When it's clear you can see as far as the Poughkeepsie Bridge." This is *my* house, I said to myself, and only I have the right to criticize it.

"Of course," he said. "I'm being obtuse. I dabble with buying and selling real estate and I see a lot of these places on the market with no takers. Costs too much to keep them up. Mine's the same. You wouldn't believe how much my coal bill was last winter. After the war we're going to subdivide into small lots and build two- and three-bedroom homes on our property. These big houses are relics."

When he saw me about to protest again he held out his hand, palm toward me. "Let me tell you about your place. Did you know two workmen were killed during the construction just before the Civil War? Around the turn of the century John Lorch bought the house—you still hear people, especially old-timers, call it the Lorch house. He was a shipbuilder, John Lorch was, famous and quite wealthy."

"Mrs. Allison said he was murdered."

"John Lorch was a bachelor and used this house to what you might call entertain. He brought women, actresses and the like, here from New York City. One of them turned out to be his downfall when she married Henry P. Schwartz. The Schwartz family was rich, but Henry was what I suppose you'd have to call unbalanced. Still, nothing would have happened if his wife hadn't confessed her affair with Lorch to her new husband."

Charles Blackstock stopped and swung his cane at a leaf on a nearby shrub. I wondered if he was thinking of his own wife.

"At a masquerade ball at the Waldorf, Schwartz, who'd been brooding on what his wife had told him, came looking for John Lorch, found him and shot him. Three times. Killed him."

"What happened to Henry Schwartz?"

"He was committed to Matteawan, a hospital for the criminally insane across the river. Might be there yet for all I know. When the police came here to close the Lorch house, your house now, they found he'd done the whole place over, the lights, the furnishings, to create an atmosphere for, ah, love. That was long ago, of course, yet it seemed to leave a mark like the mark of Cain on the house—a stain, if you believe that sort of thing."

"I don't," I said. Charles Blackstock smiled. "Here, Anne, let me help." He took the end of the tape and with Charles calling out the distances while I recorded them in my notebook, we were soon finished.

"You're an efficient girl," he said. I smiled, knowing he meant to compliment me.

"Come with me," he said. "I'd like to show you my place." He saw me hesitate. "Don't worry about Brutus," he said. "You won't even see him."

"All right," I told him. "Give me five minutes." My loafers were soaked from the wet grass.

I changed to a pair of dry ankle socks and put on another pair of shoes. When I rejoined Charles he led me to a path from the side of my house to the fence where, hidden behind syringa bushes, there was a stile.

He saw me look along the fence. "Jeremy locked Brutus up before he left for work," he said. So Jeremy wasn't home. Why did I feel so disappointed? Charles held my hand and I climbed to the top of the stile, turned, and descended the other side backward. Charles followed me over with the agility of a much younger man. Bushes grew close to the foot of the stile on the Blackstone side.

"So the dog can't make a run to leap over," Charles said. "He's Jeremy's dog, raised him from a pup." He brushed off his pants. He wore a black suit with a gold watch chain looped from his vest to his watchpocket. "A Doberman makes a good watchdog," he said. "No one bothers you when you have a Doberman. You should get a dog—two women alone in that big house."

"I guess I'm more of a cat person," I said.

We reached the two columns framing the Blackstocks' front entrance. This, then, I thought, was the world as seen by the Blackstocks. I looked from the porch to the front yard, where the pines shut off any view of the village, over the fence to my house and then to the rear where the lawn began its sweep to the river. I decided I wouldn't like being cut off from the rest of the world as the Blackstocks were.

"Sometimes I feel isolated here," Charles said as though he read my thoughts. "Like being on an island in a way. Of course, we're used to the place after all these years." He opened the large front door. "But let me show you the house, or at least the first floor. That's the only part we have furnished."

The rooms were dark—leather and mahogany rooms with thick carpets, drawn drapes across entire walls, brick hearths, mounted birds and animal heads. Rooms, I thought, designed by men for men.

"I saved this for last," he said. "My study." I watched dust motes drift in the late morning sun slanting from the high windows to the beige carpet. A pipe rack sat on a cluttered desk; magazines lay scattered on tables and on the floor. Four glass-enclosed gun cases were arranged in a rectangular pattern on the wall to my left. A narrow case in the center contained a bonehandled knife with a blade that must have been nine inches long. A deer head stared with large sad eyes from above the fireplace; open shelves of books filled an entire wall. On another wall two maps were mounted and, when I examined them, I found one was of France, the other of the South Pacific, both with clusters of pins marking the war's battle lines. The room reminded me of my father's den in the house at the lake.

"I like your study," I told Charles. "Very much." I glanced at the magazines. *Street and Smith Western, True West, Dime Western.* On the covers gunmen dueled with smoking six-shooters, bandits ambushed stagecoaches and Indian war parties circled covered wagons.

"My secret vice," Charles Blackstock said. "I can't seem to get my fill of Westerns." I tried to picture him in the Old West but couldn't. Wait. Yes, I could see him—a judge glaring down from the bench. "He's hard, Judge Blackstock," I imagined one cowboy, his foot on the saloon rail, saying to another, "but he's fair."

"I've never read Western stories," I told him. "When I was younger, though, I used to go to Western movies on Saturday afternoons to see Tom Mix, Buck Jones, Hopalong Cassidy."

He nodded. "Please sit down," he said and I sank into an armchair. I liked the firm feel of the leather on my fingers. Charles gestured to the bookcases. "Zane

Grey, Luke Short—fact or fiction, I've got them all."
He walked to a table beyond the fireplace. "Can I interest
you in a drink?" he asked, looking down at an array
of bottles. I shook my head and watched while Charles
poured one for himself. "Brandy," he said, holding the
glass to the light.

He sat across from me. "Ahhh," he said as he sipped.
"One of the few pleasures left me. Doc Dempsey can't
seem to abide seeing a man enjoy himself." He saw
me looking at the guns on the wall. "Don't be alarmed,"
he said, "if you hear shooting. I keep my pistols in working order and go down by the river for target practice.
People around here are used to hearing me, but even so
I try to shoot while they're at work. You teach, don't
you?"

I nodded.

"The schools, I don't understand them," he said.
"Maybe you'd be able to help, have some influence.
They teach Greek myths, Roman myths, legends written
in an English you can't even read. Yet they ignore the
myths and legends of their own country, of their own
time. The West! Within my lifetime the West has become
a myth. Think of it—an industrial civilization in conflict
with a primitive one, the iron horse, the gunfighter as
the archetypal hero. Magnificent."

"I teach mathematics," I said. I shouldn't have said
anything, I thought. Charles looked at me as though
he had forgotten I was in the room.

"Well, you wouldn't be much help then. Did you
know I once met Bat Masterson? Twenty-five years
ago. He worked for a New York newspaper at the time
and when I went to their office a young man came over
to me. 'Dino's,' he said, 'he's probably down the street
at Dino's.' Sure enough he was. I introduced myself
and offered to buy him a drink.

"'A brandy flip,' he said. 'Try one. The egg makes
all the difference.'

"Bat Masterson. Can you imagine? He knew Wyatt
Earp, Doc Holliday, all the great gunfighters. And I
shook Bat Masterson's hand and he told me about the

old days, seemed to want to. I didn't push. Mostly he talked 'bout his brother Ed who was killed in Dodge City. 'I held Ed's head on my lap,' he said, 'and bawled like a baby.' "

Charles Blackstock sat for a long time without speaking, staring at the empty fireplace. At last he shook his head and got up and placed his empty glass on the table. As I started to leave the room I noticed an alcove by the door and inside, on a shelf, an enlarged snapshot of a man with his arm around the waist of a short black-haired woman.

I looked quickly away, but Charles walked past me and held the picture out to me by its silver frame. "Recognize me?" he asked. "This was when we were first married." He stood looking at the picture and when he spoke there was a catch in his voice. "Gerry was a mighty pretty woman," he said.

"Geraldine?" I asked, ill at ease. I wondered why Mrs. Allison said she looked like me—I saw no resemblance.

"Yes. She named Jeremy after herself. 'Jeremy, my Jerry,' she used to say." He returned the picture to the shelf. "I loved her very much," he said in a low voice. He took out his watch and wound the stem. "Jeremy took it hard when she left. My fault, I suppose. I tried to explain to him, told him she wasn't all to blame, but how do you tell a boy about those things, what's between a man and his wife?"

We walked to the stile without talking. "Come again," he said, "now that you know the way." He helped me climb the ladderlike steps. "Call first. I'll see that Brutus is locked up." I left him standing on his side of the fence. I didn't look back, but I felt his eyes follow me all the way to my porch.

I was sorry for him, but a suspicion nagged at me. As if Charles Blackstock wasn't all he appeared to be, that behind his friendly manner he was someone who had let me know exactly what he wanted me to know. Anne, Anne, I told myself, you're becoming as cynical as Don Nevins.

A bike rested on its kickstand in front of my porch. Carroll Johnson sat on the steps. "I didn't realize it was so late," I told him. "Let me show you what I'd like you to do today." I started him off raking leaves along the Blackstock fence.

After a lunch of tomato soup and a peanut butter sandwich I went back outside. The midday sun was warm so I left my sweater on a porch chair and went down the steps to the driveway. Footsteps approached from the side of the house. Carroll must be done already, I thought.

"Come around to the front," I called, "and I'll help you clean the gutters."

"I'm really not dressed for gutter cleaning."

I stepped back and looked up into dark brown eyes. Jeremy.

# Chapter 8

Jeremy was right, he wasn't dressed for cleaning gutters. He wore white slacks, a white sport shirt open at the neck and brown-and-white shoes, the clothes emphasizing his wavy black hair and dark face.

"I thought you were Carroll Johnson," I said.

His eyes narrowed—strange eyes, so dark a brown as to appear almost black. Then he smiled, the smile of a man performing an unaccustomed ritual. "My father said he'd met you and had you over to visit."

"Yes. I liked your house, especially the study. A man's kind of room."

"I'm surprised. Or are you just being polite?" His voice was sharp with suspicion.

"I wouldn't say I liked something if I didn't." I was annoyed. "Probably I like the study because of my father. We were close, my father and I, before he died." Did I really want to reveal so much of myself to Jeremy?

I changed the subject. "I'm planning to remodel my house," I said.

"Father told me. I'm afraid I agree with him. I think you'd be better off if you sold and moved into a smaller place."

"So you and he can build two- and three-bedroom houses here after the war?" Why must I jab at him as though reconnoitering an enemy position? I expected him to protest his innocence, but he did not.

"Will you go dancing with me tonight?" he asked.

"I . . . I . . . " I could think of nothing to say, for whatever I may have expected from Jeremy Blackstock it was not a dancing invitation. To hide my confusion, I looked away. I heard Carroll whistle as he raked leaves by the fence and, over the tops of the autumn-hued trees, I saw the river sparkle in the sunlight. A freighter, low in the water, plowed southward toward the sea.

"You aren't busy tonight, are you?" he asked.

"No," I said, even more flustered. I was in full retreat. "I'm not, as a matter of fact, but you're asking me on Saturday afternoon to . . . "

"Are you the sort of woman," he interrupted, "who follows all the petty protocols? Who doesn't answer an invitation without first consulting her *Emily Post?* I'd like you to go dancing with m  Will you?"

I drew a deep breath. "Yes,  I said. Jeremy had overrun my defenses.

"Good. I'll call for you around seven-thirty." His fingers pressed the back of my hand, then he turned and strode away. My skin tingled from his touch.

I saw Jeremy stop and talk to Carroll, the boy holding his rake in one hand while he gestured with the other, nodding and laughing at something Jeremy said. Even my allies were deserting me. The white cat stretched and walked confidently along the narrow porch rail while he watched me with complacent scorn. MacArthur, I thought, don't look at me like that. Remember you lost your first battles, too.

After supper I corrected ninth-grade papers before I went through the clothes in my closet and selected the black cocktail dress. The scoop neckline, while not immodest, was startling with its contrast of black silk and white me. Will he like the dress? I wondered. As I fastened the rhinestone necklace I examined myself in the mirror.

I gave my face a passing grade, about a seventy-five, the comfortable face of your best friend's sister. My brown hair curled to my shoulders—eighty-five. Figure? I was no Betty Grable, but neither was I the spinster schoolteacher. Not yet anyway. Ninety was probably too high, though. Another eighty-five, I decided.

When I was ready, I sat in my rocker marking red X's through incorrect answers on geometry quizzes. Seven-thirty came, went, and the minute hand edged to twenty before eight. I was impatient, irked; yet underneath I felt the gnaw of panic, the fear he wouldn't come. I laid the papers aside and looked from the window toward the Blackstock house. I could see no one in the lowering dusk.

The door chimes rang at seven forty-five. I went down the stairs, my coat over one arm, relief mingling with an annoyance at Jeremy for exposing my insecurity. "Come in," I called, pausing a few steps from the bottom. He opened the door and looked up at me. I waited for his reaction, but he gave none, merely nodded, his face immobile.

"Do you think I'll need the coat?" I asked after a moment.

"Yes, you will."

"Well, I don't know. The weather is almost like Indian summer. I don't think I'll take the coat after all; it's so much bother. A sweater will do." I hung the coat on the rack in the hall. When I turned I found Jeremy glaring at me, his face tight.

"I don't care if you wear the coat or not," he said. "But the next time you ask my opinion at least give it some consideration."

I looked at him in surprise. What was he talking about? Did he think I'd asked him whether to wear the coat and then spurned his advice? Was he going to take everything I said literally? The evening was turning into a disaster before it began. I got the coat and handed it to him without a word, slipping my arms into the sleeves. As he smoothed the fur collar on my shoulders his fingers brushed my hair. I busied myself with the buttons so he wouldn't notice my quick smile of pleasure.

Jeremy held the door of his Cadillac for me, then walked behind the car to the driver's seat. The evening sky was still light in the west, but a single star shone over the trees to the east.

"We'll go by way of Shore Drive," he said. We drove down the long hill to the river, where Jeremy turned left on a road paralleling the railroad tracks. Ahead of us I saw the red light of the last car of a passenger train. Jeremy speeded up and when I glanced at him I saw his eyes fixed on the train, his fingers clenched on the steering wheel. We drew even with the last coach, passed it, then slowly went by one lighted car after another, so close I could make out the expressions on the passengers' faces.

Ahead of us the engine billowed smoke and in the distance I saw the arms of a warning sign where the road crossed the tracks. Jeremy pressed on the accelerator, making gravel beat against our fenders. He drove faster and faster until fear knotted my stomach and I gripped the armrest, my body rigid. The car came even with the locomotive and for a moment neither gained. We were head to head—the train, car and crossing seemed to converge; and then we spurted forward, swerved, bumped over the tracks with the locomotive's headlight flashing into my eyes. Jeremy slowed. The train was a receding rumble behind us.

I slumped back in the seat and turned to make a biting remark only to find Jeremy smiling a smile of triumph. I bit my lip and remained silent. We drove on, neither of us speaking. We had not, I realized, spoken since we left the house and I began to feel uncomfortable. The silence wasn't easy or companionable—rather, it stretched taut between us.

We passed a sign: ENTERING THE CITY OF NEWBURGH.

"I like Canterbury High School," I said, knowing I sounded inane.

"Good," he said.

"I understand you lettered at Canterbury."

"Yes, and we played the championship basketball game here in Newburgh. During my senior year."

"Did you go on to college?" I was beginning to be desperate as each of my attempts at conversation foundered on his laconic replies.

"Not right away, and then only for two years. The war came along and I enlisted."

"Don't you miss it?"

"The war?"

"No, before the war, when you played basketball. The crowds, the excitement."

"Yes, sometimes I do. Not often, though. That part of my life seems to belong to another time, like it all happened to some other Jeremy Blackstock, not to me."

Our car jounced over a cobblestone street to the ferry station where we waited in a line of cars while a ferry docked in one of the slips.

"I guess I've become something of a misanthrope," Jeremy said. "I enjoy and guard my privacy. When I played ball the worst part was the reporters and their questions, questions, always the same questions. I used to skip reading the writeups of our games in the *Local* because I didn't like to see my name in print. Now I think of all that as the past. There must be more important ways to spend your life than scoring baskets."

I thought of his race with the train and wondered how much he had changed, but I didn't comment. "What *do* you want?" I asked.

"I don't know. Rather late in life, twenty-nine, not to know. Right now I'm doing translations, German to English, English to German. I spoke both languages when I was growing up."

"And wrote two, one with each hand?"

"Oh, that's just a parlor trick. Who told you?"

"Mrs. Allison," I said.

Cars disembarking from the ferry passed us one after the other, lights on, and passengers walked from the terminal building to the parking lot and to the bus station next door.

"Anne," Jeremy said, "I worry about you in that old house with only Mrs. Allison. She's getting on and doesn't hear well any more. Besides, I have a bad feeling about your place. I remember when I was a boy your house was vacant a lot and I used to lie in bed at night and look across at that great old mansion, the Lorch house we called it then, and I'd imagine I saw lights flicker inside and conjure up faces at the windows. I don't know how I can convince you, except I feel there's a wrongness about the place."

I sensed an urgency in his voice. But was his concern for me? "I'm not afraid," I said. "What is there to be afraid of?"

"I wish I knew, but I don't. I just know I'd feel a lot better if you lived someplace else."

Could Jeremy have invited me out tonight merely to persuade me to leave my new home? "I've been from attic to cellar," I said, trying to keep my voice light. "There are no ghosts." I had a moment of disquiet when I remembered the unlocked door, but said nothing.

Jeremy was about to speak when our line of cars began to move. He shifted and drove up the incline onto the ferry, where a white-haired man directed us to the left lane. A whistle shrilled, the gate clanged shut and the boat shuddered away from the pilings of the dock.

"We'll go on deck," Jeremy said. He opened my door and held my arm to guide me between parked cars to the stairs. The upper deck was open, deserted; the river was to our right, the wheelhouse above on the left. Wind stung my face and pulled at my hair so I tied a scarf over my head. I was glad I had worn my coat.

"Cigarette?" Jeremy asked. When I shook my head he cupped his hand to light his own and I smelled the tobacco smoke mingled with the odors of the river. I

saw another ferry, aglow with lights, approach from
the far shore. Downstream the Hudson was dark with
the mountains black along the banks, but in the sky
a muted light promised the moon for later. Jeremy put
both hands on the rail and stared down at the water
churning away from the sides of the boat.

"What do you see?" I asked.

For a moment I thought he wasn't going to answer;
then, eyes still on the water, he spoke in a voice so
low he seemed to be talking to himself. "I see death,"
he said, and, startled, I glanced at his face, thinking
of his grandmother who had drowned herself in this
river.

I saw the spurt of steam from near the wheelhouse of
the other ferry and a few seconds later I heard the whistle. "Life seems to me like that boat going by out there,"
Jeremy said. "All alight and alive, yet after it's gone
nothing is left except a few ripples on the water, and
then nothing at all." He flipped his cigarette away and
the glowing end spun out and back along the side of the
boat into the water. "I love the river," he said softly, "always changing, always the same. She must have loved
the river, too, to want to die in it."

What a strange man, I thought. For the first time
I warmed to him, felt a sympathy—because, I told myself,
he needs someone, someone who will give meaning to
his life. The Blackstocks are cursed, Mrs. Allison had
said. What nonsense! Nothing as simple as a curse af-
flicted Jeremy. He had retreated rather than meeting life
head on. He needed affection, a new beginning, someone real and honest on whom he could depend.

I shook my head. All day, I realized, I had been
posing—making my meeting with Jeremy in the morning
into something like a military encounter, rating myself
in the mirror, pausing on the stairs to invite his compliment. I had been false and unreal, not at all the person
I wanted to be.

Impulsively I slid my hand along the rail, found
Jeremy's and twined my fingers with his. Jeremy looked
at me, surprised, his eyes black, masked. Then he gripped

my hand tightly, and we stood looking at one another, not speaking.

With a crunch the boat, slowing, scraped the pilings of the Beacon dock and I saw a crewman poised with a mooring line ready to throw ashore. I took off my scarf and as the wind tousled my hair I felt a new awareness, an anticipation—I was ready to believe the past could be left stored in trunks in the attic, that pumpkins do change into coaches, mice into coachmen. I was experiencing, I thought, a sea change into something rich and strange.

The ferry docked, the gate swung open and we joined the line of cars streaming ashore. I was alive, intoxicated. Jeremy talked, I talked, there seemed to be so much to say. A barrier between us had burst and the past seemed swept aside, if only for tonight.

We left the car in a parking lot. "We're going up Mount Beacon," Jeremy told me. "The cogwheel train goes every hour to the dance pavilion at the summit."

The cogwheel train climbed slowly. It's like the beginning of a roller-coaster ride, I thought, with the undulating mountains for our roller coaster. Soon we were above the trees and, seeing the river shimmer to the west, I realized the moon must have risen behind us. At the summit we walked toward the light shining from the large windows of the pavilion. Music rose and fell on the night air.

The moon, full and luminous, hung suspended over the mountains, silvering the trees, the river, the couples laughing on the balcony. In the moonlight the women were radiant, beautiful; the men, mostly in uniform, were dark and dashing. While the stars above our heads seemed almost within reach, the lights of Beacon below us were dim, and Newburgh, winking from across the river, was a distant, foreign land.

"Canterbury's over there," Jeremy said, nodding to the south, but I could see nothing except a scattering of lights amidst the hills and mountains.

We danced. Jeremy seemed taller and he danced smoothly, led with confidence and a sure sense of rhythm.

The band played the old songs, the slow sentimental songs—"Smoke Gets in Your Eyes," "To Each His Own," "You Made Me Love You," and I hummed, removed from time, without a past or a future, content to have Jeremy's arms about me, his body against mine, his face lightly touching my hair.

A female vocalist in a strapless red gown stood before the microphone. "Moonlight Becomes You," she sang. "My request," Jeremy murmured in my ear. "But it's not just because there's moonlight," he said. After the dance we walked from the crowded room to the balcony, where we stood side by side high above the valley.

"Look." Jeremy pointed to the sky. I saw a shooting star streak earthward and fade to nothingness. A wish, a wish, make a wish. I wished for a lifetime of moments like this.

"Let's walk," I suggested, and we strolled along a pathway leading away from the pavilion. We walked until the lights were only a glow behind us and the murmur of voices stilled. I began to talk; I told Jeremy of myself and college, about my father and the trip he and I had taken after my mother died, of my father's death and the umbrellas in the rain. I told him my fears, my hopes. When I finished I felt empty, yet at peace.

Jeremy took my hand and we walked back to the ballroom. "We have time for one more dance," he said. Already? Why must the evening end so soon? His arm held me tighter and I danced close to him, content and happy.

We caught the last car down the mountain. Jeremy drove south through the deserted after-midnight streets of small towns, crossed the bridge at Bear Mountain, and, as we followed the curving road around the mountains to Canterbury, the sound and motion of the car lulled me and I dozed. I woke to find my head on his shoulder. I smiled, nestling closer to him; I felt his hand hold me to him.

He walked with me up the porch steps. At the top I turned and he held both of my hands in his. "I can't remember," I told him, "when I've had such a wonderful

evening." He leaned to me and his hands moved to
my back, his face inches from mine, and I knew he
would kiss me and I shut my eyes. His hands tightened,
his lips brushed my forehead and he stepped back.

"Good night," he whispered and walked from the
porch into the moonlight. I unlocked the door and stood
inside by the glass panels watching the headlights of
his car go down the driveway. Humming, I ran up the
stairs to my room.

Karl's picture regarded me with suspicion from the
nightstand. I ignored him. Even though the clock said
ten after three I was wide awake.

When I was ready for bed I turned out the lights
and looked from the window toward the Blackstocks'.
Did I glimpse someone walking on the slope above the
river? I peered into the darkness, but nothing moved. I
sat in the rocker staring out at the silhouettes of the trees.

I remembered riding on a train as a child, probably
when Father and I moved from one town to another
after he'd sold the latest of his many businesses. Before
I went to sleep I watched the telegraph poles flicking
by the window of the Pullman and saw the monotonous
reaches of flat farmland.

In the morning when I woke the train was stopped
and I looked out at a street in what appeared to be
a fairy-tale village with snow piled on the steep roofs,
icicles hanging from the eaves, villagers bundled in heavy
coats, their breath coming in white plumes. I wanted to
dress and run from the train into the village street.

My breath misted the window of the train. When
I wiped it clear with the sleeve of my nightgown I looked
beyond the street. Evergreens huddled around the town
and just past the trees steep cliffs rose black and sheer;
crags loomed above. My delight changed as a cold and
ominous feeling grew in me. I thought the men and
women looked fearfully about them and hurried to seek
shelter. Snow on one of the roofs slid down, soundlessly,
to the street, sending a whirlwind of crystals into the
air. The train lurched ahead and in a few minutes the

village was gone, left forever behind. Lovely? En-
chanted? Evil?

I slipped into bed, pushing down my uneasiness. What
a strange thing to remember tonight, I thought. I bunched
the pillow under my head and deliberately reviewed
the events of the evening. I thought of Jeremy, imagined
him touching me, wondered how I would feel when
he kissed me—for I knew he would. I thought of the
ferry ride, the dances on the mountaintop, the falling
star. You're too romantic, Anne, I told myself. Yet
I knew wishes could come true.

I sensed Karl's accusing stare, so I laid his picture
face down on the nightstand, turned over and went to
sleep.

# Chapter 9

The door chimes woke me. How long had they been
ringing? Mrs. Allison must be in the back of the house
where she can't hear them, I thought. I slid into my
slippers, pulled on my quilted robe and hurried to the
bedroom door. The door was open—not much, a few
inches, but open. My stomach knotted. Last night I
had been so elated, the hour so late, had I remembered
to lock the door? I was sure I had. I felt as I did when
I neglected a toothache and congratulated myself when
it went away only to wake in the night with a throbbing
pain.

The chimes rang again. My mind in a turmoil, I ran
down the stairs, swung open the front door and looked
out expecting to see Jeremy.

"Why, Don," I said, hoping my disappointment didn't
show. He wore a plaid black-and-red jacket and brown
shorts. He held a tennis racket in his hand.

"Did I wake you?" he asked. He looked at his wrist-
watch. "It's nine-thirty; I thought you'd be dressed.

I tried to call, but they don't have your number and I forgot the name of the lady who lives downstairs so I thought I'd just stop by to see if you'd like to play a couple of sets like we said last week." Don's words came with a rush.

"I was just surprised," I said. "I wasn't expecting you."

"I'm sorry if I got you up."

"It's all right, Don, come into the hall. Yes, I'll play if you'll wait. I won't be long."

I left him sitting on the bench beside the grandfather clock with the racket between his knees. After a quick bath I put on my white linen blouse, white shorts and red sweater. Next to the white of the shorts my legs still seemed to have their midsummer tan. I found my racket in the closet, unscrewed the press and laid it on my unmade bed.

I made sure I set the lock on my way out. Either I had forgotten to lock the door last night, which was unlikely, or I had unlocked it in my sleep. That seemed even more bizarre, for I had never been a sleepwalker. Had someone deliberately sought to frighten me? But why? And where had they gotten the key?

I wished I had someone to talk to. Jeremy? Already the ferry, the moonlight, the ride home in the early morning seemed unreal and dreamlike. And I thought I knew what Jeremy would tell me. Leave the house, Anne; rent an apartment near the school. He'd listen to me explain why I didn't want to leave, and then he'd say, "Why do you ask my advice if you don't intend to follow it?" Couldn't men understand we didn't want them to tell us what to do, but wanted them to support and maybe even applaud what we've already decided?

Don stood up as I came down the stairs. "You look awfully pretty," he said. "So fresh and wholesome."

I smiled. All I could think of was a loaf of bread. But instead of fresh I felt at least a week old and stale. What had Jeremy said last night while we danced? "Moonlight becomes you?" I smiled at the memory.

"A penny for your thoughts." I started. Don was looking down at me as he held the front door.

"Just daydreaming," I said.

Don's car was in the drive; it was an Austin two-seater. As we drove past the Blackstock house I saw Brutus lope across the lawn and I thought I glimpsed someone coming from under the pines. Jeremy? I turned my head so he wouldn't see me looking at him.

The two tennis courts were next to the creek behind the high school. Four boys played on the near one, but the second court was deserted. "Two sets?" Don asked. I nodded.

Don, playing an awkward yet determined game, won the first, 6-3. We both began to tire in the second. I led at set point when he rushed the net and I lobbed the ball far over his head. Too far, for it bounced a few inches behind the backcourt line.

"Good," he called, "you win."

"Wasn't the ball out?"

"It was on the line." I thought I saw him blush. "One set each, we'll play the tie-breaker another day."

We walked to the path leading along the creek to look for a lost ball.

"Anne," he said, "if you ever need anything, just let me know."

"Why, what do you mean?"

He looked uncomfortable. "Those neighbors of yours, the Blackstocks. I've heard some rather strange stories about them."

"You've been asking people." I looked accusingly at him.

"Only because I'm concerned." He reddened. "For you," he added. "The father, is Charles his name?" I nodded. "They say his wife claimed he acted, well, peculiar. Of course, that was just before she left him."

"What do you mean, peculiar?"

"She said he was, I don't know how to put it, well, odd—and brutal to her."

"Just gossip. From what I've heard, she was the one who was kind of unstable."

"And Jeremy, his son," Don went on. "People say they meet him on the mountain, in the glen, along the river, always alone, and he nods and walks on, never stopping to pass the time of day. Takes after his father, keeps to himself . . . "

"I don't want to hear any more," I told him.

"All right, but remember what I said, if there's ever anything I can . . . "

"Look, there's the ball on the other side of the creek."

"A brook 'too broad for leaping,' " he quoted.

"Do you like Housman?" I asked.

"One of my favorites." Don stepped from rock to rock until he reached the far bank, where he retrieved the ball.

"He's gloomy, but I like him too," I said. We climbed the hill and walked across the soccer field to his car. The day was warm; the sun came in and out from behind white puffs of cloud. We stopped at Santoro's for a Coke and Don talked about the school, the students and the teachers. I relaxed and told him my problem with the math club. He shook his head.

"Why don't you give up?" he asked. "Spend the time and effort on something else. It's not worth while for just three students; not worth the hassle."

"No, I can't, not yet. I'll think of some way to make the club go."

"Good luck. I hope you do." He's an easy man to be with, I thought. I could tell he liked me in his awkward, determined way. Why then, though I enjoyed talking to him and would have liked to know him better, did I feel that if he touched me in a man-woman way he might mar the tenuous relation we had?

"What?" I asked. I hadn't been listening.

"At times," he repeated, "I think I'm the kind of person who would prefer mourning a lost love to having a real one."

I raised my eyebrows. "More Housman?" I asked.

"Must be," he said, getting up. He left me at my front porch. "Again soon?" he asked.

"Yes, I'd like to. The phone's listed under Mrs. Allison's name."

"Allison," he repeated. "I'll remember. I'll do better—I'll write the name down." He was leaning on his car writing on a piece of paper when I went inside.

On Sunday afternoon I marked papers and prepared lesson plans for the coming week. I found school a necessary relief from the uneasiness I felt in the house, yet I worried about whether I could give my full attention to the job. I had become acquainted with some of the teachers, especially Jean and Charley. They were both women—Charley was Charlene. They shared an apartment across from the school and on Tuesdays I lunched with them. As we ate our hard-boiled eggs Jean talked home economics and Charley, girls' physical education, to the accompaniment of records on the phonograph.

Jeremy called me on Wednesday evening. "I didn't want you to think I always waited till the last minute to ask for a date," he said.

"Oh?" I answered as I tried to keep the excitement from my voice.

"Would you go to the show with me in Newburgh on Friday night? *Going My Way* with Bing Crosby and Barry Fitzgerald. You haven't seen it, have you?"

"No, and I want to. The reviews were good."

"Six o'clock. We can eat on the way."

After I put down the receiver I ran upstairs. I felt like singing. All week I had denied the attraction I felt for Jeremy Blackstock; I had attempted to dismiss last Saturday night as unreal. I no longer could.

My euphoric mood even survived the dismal Thursday afternoon meeting of the faithful three members of the mathematics club. From outside we could hear the thud of soccer balls as the team practiced on the playground behind the school. I must do something for the math club or I'll have failed, I told myself as I trudged home. But what?

Mrs. Allison met me on the front porch. From the smile on her face I could tell she had good news to share. "He called," she said.

"Who?"

"Why, the major. He'll arrive tomorrow afternoon. You did remember you're going to have dinner with us, didn't you? I'm so looking forward to your meeting him."

"Yes, of course," I said. "I remembered."

I was halfway up the stairs to my bedroom when I realized what I had done. Oh my God, I thought, I told Jeremy I'd go to the movies with him on Friday. I'd forgotten that was the day the major was coming.

No one answered when I called the Blackstock number. Finally, on my fourth call at eight o'clock, I heard Jeremy's voice. When I told him about the dinner with Mrs. Allison and her son there was a long silence. "All right," he said at last, "I understand. We'll go another time."

"Why don't we—" I began—then I heard the phone click. Tears stung my eyes. I had the sudden urge to call him back. To tell him what? Didn't he think I was telling the truth? I dabbed at my eyes and blew my nose with my handkerchief. The major would probably be the most dashing man I'd ever met.

# Chapter 10

The major arrived on schedule. When I entered the dining room at six-thirty his back was to me. A pipe in his hand, he gestured at his mother, who was carrying dishes from the kitchen.

"Just a foolish Scottish superstition," he said. "You shouldn't worry."

"You can call it foolish if you want," Mrs. Allison said, "but the last time one fell old Mrs. McLaughlin was dead within forty-eight hours."

"Oh," the major said, turning and seeing me. "I'm sorry." He had a narrow moustache and wore an Eisenhower jacket, four rows of multicolored ribbons and a gold band on the third finger of his left hand. David Niven, I thought. A married David Niven.

"You must be Anne Medford."

"Yes, Major Allison, I am."

"You're too pretty to be . . . "

"A math teacher." I said the last words along with him.

"You've heard that before." He smiled, drew on his pipe. "You don't mind?" I shook my head as he held up the pipe. "My wife taught fourth grade," he said, "before we were married."

"Mrs. Allison didn't mention her."

"Mildred. She lives in Santa Cruz eighty miles south of San Francisco. At the beginning of the war we tried having her follow me from army post to army post, but it became a succession of late trains, waiting in bus stations, and crowded army towns with no place to live. When I was sent to England we decided she'd stay with her mother and father for the duration."

Mrs. Allison finished placing the food on the table. The major held her chair for her.

"Mother's worried," he told me after we said grace.

"Don't exaggerate," she said. "He likes to tease me," she said to me.

"You are worried, you know you are." He looked at me, smiling. "This afternoon the big picture of Robert Burns in the living room fell from the wall for no apparent reason. According to the Scots this means someone close to us will die. Not only die, but within the week."

"We'll see if you're still scoffing seven days from now," Mrs. Allison said. "Take some more," she said to me. She had cooked roast beef and Yorkshire pudding.

"My favorite meal," the major said. "You know, Mother, even in London I couldn't get Yorkshire pudding as good as yours." When his mother smiled at him I saw the resemblance between the two. He was a thin, precise-looking man only slightly taller than I.

"What time do you want to go in the morning?" he asked his mother.

"Eight o'clock?"

"Fine. I'll be glad to see Aunt Edna again." He treated his mother, I thought, with a fond forbearance. The major turned to me. "My aunt lives on Long Island a few miles from where the World's Fair was held."

"My father and I went to the fair in 1939," I said. "I still remember the bus horns playing the first part of 'Sidewalks of New York,' the frozen custard—I'd never had any before—the trylon and perisphere. . . ."

"The lighted fountain show at night," the major broke in, "the General Motors exhibit, the parachute jump . . ."

"I'll never forget one ride," I said. "A roller coaster. Not like the ordinary ones where you're pulled to the top of a long straight incline. This roller coaster climbed a huge open funnel and began going down inside in big, slow swoops, and as we went the cars speeded up, moved faster and faster, the circles got smaller and I clung to the rail in front of me and we shot ahead faster yet—until I knew if we rounded one more curve the car would leave the tracks and hurl us all into space!"

"I'd have enjoyed that ride," the major said.

"Wine?" Mrs. Allison asked.

"Wizard," the major said. I took a glass and we sat in the parlor while the major talked of England, last year's preparations for the invasion, the air raids and the destruction in the cities, the German rocket attacks. My troubles seemed insignificant compared to what our men overseas were enduring, and I felt ashamed of myself, of my pettiness and my selfishness.

Mrs. Allison got up. "I have to finish packing," she said.

"Will you take a stroll with me?" the major asked.

"Yes, I'd like to. Let me run upstairs for a sweater."

The major waited in the front hall surrounded by the aroma of his tobacco. He held the door for me and we walked around to the back of the house, where we stood looking down at the river. Lights from a ship moved slowly toward the north.

"I'd think Mother would get lonely here," he said, "with just the two houses set off by themselves; and

from what she says the people next door, the, the . . ."
He groped for the name.

"Blackstocks."

"Yes, the Blackstocks. She says they aren't too
neighborly. But she likes the house; seems to be getting
along famously." As we walked on in silence I buttoned
my sweater against the wind off the water.

"Only seven miles from West Point," he said. "It's
a wonder the Germans have never tried to land men
from a sub along the river. They did, you know, on
Long Island in the first year of the war, put four spies
ashore. They were at large for weeks before they were
caught."

"Do you think they would, here?"

"No, unlikely. Don't let my military imagination upset
you. Probably there are nets and all sorts of other anti-
submarine devices downriver in New York harbor. I'm
surprised, though, that the civil defense people are getting
so complacent. Has there been a practice blackout
lately?"

"Not for months, I understand."

He shook his head. "Oh, I'm sorry, are you cold?"
He had seen me shiver.

"A little."

"Come on, we'll head away from the river." We went
through the yard and onto Spruce Street.

"Has Mother been acting all right?" he asked.

I looked at him with surprise. "Why yes, she seems
fine to me."

"I've been worried about her since Neal died," he
said. "My younger brother—only brother actually. He
was killed at Anzio."

"I'm sorry." So much death. I didn't like to hear of
death.

"Mother never cried. At first she seemed to be in
a daze, never mentioned Neal, went on as though nothing
had happened. Then she began to think people were
talking about her behind her back, that somehow they
had something to do with Neal's death. She's harmless,
of course. I bought her the two cats, MacArthur and To-

jo. They've helped, I think, and having you in the house has been good for her. She sounded worried in the letters she wrote before you arrived, but not since. You seem to be a level-headed young woman. As well as a very attractive one."

"Your mother is a good tenant," I said.

"I'm glad. As a matter of fact I tried to get her to move a year or so ago. She wouldn't hear of it. She's grown attached to the place like older people do. I'd hate to think of her having to leave."

We had reached the front door. The major held out his hand. Surprised, I hesitated, then saw he meant to shake hands with me. His grip was strong and hard. "Mother's coming back on the train Sunday night," he said. He seemed about to add something, but didn't. He held the door for me, but when I started to climb the stairs he came to the railing.

"Take this," he said, handing me a slip of paper. "If Mother ever needs me," he said, "or if you need to call me about her, this is where I can be reached." He turned and went into his mother's apartment.

As I undressed for bed I thought of what the major had said. What had he been trying to tell me? Was a second meaning hidden behind his words? I shook my head, puzzled.

After I turned out the lights I opened the drapes. I saw movement in the orchard and when I peered into the darkness I saw an animal run beneath the trees and disappear around the house. Brutus? I shivered. No, I told myself, probably a stray dog from the village.

I slid between the cool covers. After Mrs. Allison and the major left in the morning I would be alone in the house. All at once I trembled, without reason, so I raised my legs and hugged them to my body. The trembling lessened, then stopped. Tomorrow I'll help Carroll work in the yard, I told myself.

I thought of dancing with Jeremy, the ride home with my head on his shoulder, his face touching my hair. Then I was no longer in the Cadillac, it was not Jeremy beside me.

My father smiled down at me. "Not on your life," he said. "You go ahead, I'll watch." I laughed and in a few minutes looked down at him and waved. The car reached the top and began to descend—around, around, faster, faster, and the roller coaster entered the final turn while I, immobile, powerless, braced myself as the car hurtled from the tracks.

Fear surged along my legs and through my body. The fear of death.

# Chapter 11

Early the next morning a harsh throbbing sound awakened me. I pulled back the drapes with my hand, but could see nothing; then I realized the noise came from a car warming up on the driveway next to the house. The sound deepened, the motor raced and a black sedan nosed into sight over the balcony rail and moved along the drive with wisps of white puffing like smoke signals from the exhaust. The major stopped the car at the road, turned into Spruce Street and was gone.

The day was dark with lowering clouds. Leaves twirled from trees to the ground where they scudded before the wind until they were caught by shrub or fence. When I looked east above the mountains on the far side of the river, I saw a red slit in the sky bordered above and below by grey clouds. Like a surgical incision, I thought. This was a morning to go back to bed, pull the covers high and seek to recapture the surprise of waking, ready to dress for work, only to remember this was Saturday, a day when I *could* curl back within the sensuous world of near-sleep.

I thought I heard a mewing from the yard below. MacArthur? Tojo? Or my conscience reminding me I had promised Mrs. Allison to take care of the cats? And Carroll would be coming soon.

After I put bread in the toaster I returned to the bedroom, where I listened to the war news as I dressed. The Allies had advanced in the Low Countries, but the thrust of the drive into Europe appeared to be blunted and another winter of war was impending. And after Germany was defeated, Japan remained. I was tired of war.

I smelled smoke. Alarmed, I looked around the room and found smoke drifting in from the hall. Oh my God, I thought. I had forgotten the toast. I ran to the kitchen, threw the two black slices into the garbage and then sat at the table staring at the charred coils in the open toaster.

Suddenly I felt I could not go on; I saw that my weeks at Canterbury had been a succession of failures. What was the use? The results of my remodeling were meager; the house itself seemed to resist me. Night after night I woke from a troubled sleep remembering voices that whispered secrets, but, no matter how long or hard I tried, I could recall nothing of what they said. At school the math club foundered in a sea of indifference.

Karl existed in another world, a world connected to mine by a paper-thin chain of letters. Don? I liked Don, yet when I was with him I sensed no magic, no excitement. And Jeremy. Excitement, yes; but my feeling toward him was as variable as his toward me, a reaching out followed by precipitous withdrawal. I feared Jeremy—was afraid to give him the power to hurt me.

Why do I stay? I asked myself. Was I merely being stubborn, unwilling to admit defeat? He who fights and runs away, I thought.

The doorbell rang. Carroll. I led him upstairs to clear the gutters. The balcony floor was flat, the wood coated with cracked grey paint. The baluster posts of the low railing, also grey, were carved with wavelike designs.

"Don't ever lean on this, Miss Medford," Carroll said when he moved the wooden rail back and forth with his hand.

"I won't," I told him, sighing. Another job to be done. Carroll threw leaves and branches from the porch to the ground in preparation for cleaning the gutter, which was really nothing more than a depression in the balcony floor next to the rail. The gutter led to drain-holes at the corners of the roof.

I returned to my bedroom. At first I had intended to paper on top of the rose design, but when I'd trimmed off the loose edges I'd found layer after layer of paper creating bulges on the surface of the wall. So I scraped the wallpaper from the plaster with the help of a wet sponge. The covering just beneath the roses was a thick red velvet and I wondered whether this was the last memento of John Lorch's "atmosphere of love."

The books. I had forgotten those prurient books at the bottom of the bookcase. Kneeling, I removed them and, my face reddening, glanced through the pages before I carried them down the stairs into the cellar. I turned on the single hanging bulb. The furnace loomed in the center of the room. Hydra-headed black pipes suspended on metal slings and brackets jutted from the top to cross the beamed ceiling.

I touched the coiled handle of the furnace door with the tip of my finger. I found the metal warm, not hot, so I grasped the handle and lifted. The door opened with a whine. I drew back before a wave of heat. The flames murmured inside, blue-orange over the coals. The fire was almost alive, I thought; it was the pulsing heart of the house, tended by servants, demanding, consuming, never dying.

One by one I thrust the books inside. I left the door open so I could watch the covers blacken and curl in the heat, at last bursting into high yellow flames. Seeing the books burn, I felt relieved, as though I had purged the house of a symptom of evil.

While I slowly climbed the cellar stairs a worry nagged at me. I remembered the day I had arrived and noticed that the paperboy did not enter the Blackstock yard. Now I had the same feeling of something amiss, out of place. The cellar? My room? I shook my head. I did not know.

When, later, I went outside to walk to the village,

the wind pushed at my back; it was a fresh, steady wind sweeping from the east over the river into the town. My hair teased my cheeks and my jacket and skirt were molded to my body. Propelled ahead, I breathed the cool damp air, feeling alive and free. Mrs. Allison had left and for the first time the house was mine alone. The despair of a few hours before was gone and I listened joyfully to the crunch of my shoes on the gravel drive.

The thock, thock of a hammer echoed from the evergreens along the street in front of the Blackstock house. Charles knelt on the outside of his white fence, an old baseball cap on his head. When he doffed the cap to me his white hair ruffled in the wind. *CHS* was printed in orange letters across the front of his sweatshirt. When I glanced past him to the yard I felt a quick surge of anticipation, but Jeremy was not there.

"Just a few loose pickets," Charles said, pulling the cap down on his forehead with one hand while he pointed to the fence with the hammer he held in the other. "Brutus can't get through, but it doesn't hurt to be careful."

I blocked the thought of the dog from my mind. "It's a wonderful day," I said.

"A line storm coming," Charles Blackstock said. "You can tell—wind's from the east 'stead of the west like usual. We get a line storm here in Canterbury most every year around the end of September, beginning of October, when the sun crosses the equator. The wind shifts and blows in off the Atlantic. Might rain for two or three days."

"I like rain," I told him. There had been none since the squall on the day of my arrival. I nodded to Charles and walked past him toward the village.

"Going ahead with your remodeling?" he called after me.

I turned and the wind blew the hair about my eyes. "I'm getting ready to paper the big bedroom," I told him. "The other upstairs rooms are next."

I thought his mouth tightened. When I went on I had the uncomfortable sensation that he stared after me. I had an urge to turn, but did not. Not until I was out of his sight on Idylwild Avenue did I again hear the steady thock, thock of the hammer. He must want to help with the work, I realized, and, needing help, I decided to talk to him later in the week.

"Looks like rain," the butcher said while he wrapped my pork chops in glazed white paper and tied the package with string from a reel suspended over the counter.

"We're going to get a real storm," the clerk in Santoro's predicted when I paid her for the *Saturday Evening Post* and *The New Yorker*. On the way out of the store I glanced at a counter piled with games and toys. Boxed jigsaw puzzles were stacked one atop the other and, looking at the puzzles, I was, without warning, six or seven years old, sick and unable to go to school.

Mother leaned over my bed to place a breadboard on my lap. The sun made a halo of her golden hair. "I have a surprise," she said and handed me the box with a picture on the cover of white clouds in a blue sky above canals and windmills.

I remembered another day. I was older, perhaps fifteen, and the floor lamp behind me threw a yellow glow on the table. My father sat across from me, his thick fingers turning over the small pieces one by one. When his fingers stopped I glanced up to see him looking at me, sad and melancholy, and, without knowing how I knew, I sensed he was remembering something from long ago.

"I'll do the sky." I told him. He didn't seem to hear, so I repeated the words.

"Yes," he said, looking at me with a start. Once more he turned over the pieces. "Yes," he said again, "you do the sky."

I took the top box from Santoro's pile of puzzles, the picture a grotto with a series of waterfalls between wet ledges of rock. I gave the clerk another dime and set off for home with my purchases.

When I reached the house I plunged into activity to overcome a growing mood of loss and desolation. By suppertime I had finished cleaning three of my bedroom walls and had only the wall with the wood paneling left. Carroll had cleared all the drains. I paid him and he promised to return as soon as school let out on Tuesday.

After supper I climbed to the attic—Carroll had replaced the bulb—and searched through the stored furniture until I found a folded card table. Although my arms were stiff from scraping wallpaper, I carried the table to my room. When I went to the window to pull the drapes I saw that the night had closed in and the trees and mountains were only a shade darker than the sky. A lone streetlight shone above the shrubs at the front of the house. The branches of the trees did not move and the leaves were still. I felt a hush of expectation in the air.

I dumped the five hundred cardboard pieces on the table. Do I really want to work a puzzle? I asked myself. Or was I trying, as if by magic, to recreate days and feelings gone forever? A few minutes after I started to piece together the puzzle's border, though, I became absorbed in the routine of search and discovery.

The windows rattled. When I got up and lifted the drape I found the night completely dark. Wind whispered through the trees and moaned over the house. As I walked from room to room to close and fasten the windows I imagined myself outside, watching the on-and-off switching of the lights tracing my path. I remembered the cats were out, so I went to the kitchen door and called. Tojo scuttled inside to the pan of milk on the floor. Where was MacArthur? Again I called from the doorway. I thought I heard the cat mew in the darkness, but he did not come.

Mrs. Allison kept a flashlight in one of the cupboards. Shining the weak beam on the stones of the walk I followed the path around the house, calling the cat. The wind had risen—not to the steady breeze of the morning, but to a gusting wind that twisted and pulled. From high overhead came the steady hum of an airplane. I looked up into the blackness and imagined the lone pilot staring into the night as he hurried to escape the storm. "Good luck," I said under my breath.

Was that the padding of feet from the Blackstock yard? I tensed, my pulse racing. I shone the light toward the fence, fearing I would see the loping figure of Brutus. Instead I saw the tossing branches of the bushes, nothing more. I hastened back to the kitchen door. As I climbed the steps a large drop of rain struck my cheek, then another and another. A rushing sound came from the river, moved toward me through the orchard. Rain spattered my dress as the storm swept in against the house. I closed and locked the door.

Tojo had left his milk to pace back and forth across the kitchen floor. He stalked to the outer door and I could see his black hair bristle and his back arch.

"What's wrong?" I asked. I looked out the window, but saw only the slanting rain. I knelt beside the cat, stroked his dark fur. He purred and rubbed his body along my leg. Strange, I thought—Tojo had never offered affection before. Lifting him to my arms I went upstairs and sat in my rocker with the cat on my lap. He moved restlessly and several times I felt his body stiffen and his head lift as though he heard sounds I could not hear. I became uneasy and my eyes darted from shape to shape in the room as I tried to pierce the gloom.

I turned on the radio, but static crackled above the music. I was surprised, for no lightning accompanied the rain. Could the interference come from the aerial whipping in the wind? I switched off the set, picked up the *Post* and began to read.

The cat's head jerked up. I didn't hear the sound at first, so intermingled was it with the howl of the wind and the slash of rain on the siding of the house. A steady wail like the keening of a bereft woman. A shiver ran along my legs and up my back. The rain. The wailing. Dark images of wet, encroaching forms seemed to grow funguslike in my mind.

I laid Tojo on the bed and walked to the window. The wailing came from without. I pushed open the window, feeling the chill of rain on my hand. The sound was louder and came, I thought, from the village. A warning of fire in the night? No, more constant, more insistent than any fire alarm.

Of course, I should have known—the air-raid siren. The signal for a blackout. I smiled wanly to myself. The major would be pleased. As though in confirmation the dim circle of the streetlight faded and was gone. I remembered I had left the light on in the kitchen. Luckily I had brought the flashlight with me. Using it to find my way in the house that was still strange to me, I returned to the first floor, flicked off the light and made my way back to the bedroom. I turned off the light and pulled the drapes open.

In a few minutes my eyes grew accustomed to the darkness, but there was little I could see. The furniture, now almost unrecognizable, crouched around me. Drops of water spotted the windows. Outside there were no rifts in the clouds, none at all, and no lights shone from the Blackstock house or from the village. In the dark the storm sounded louder, more threatening, as the wind and rain drove onto the metal roof and against the clapboards as if to probe for a crack, a loose board, any infirmity in the aging house.

I heard a scraping—like the noise Brutus made when he clawed on the Blackstocks' fence. My hands gripped the knobs on the arms of the chair as my ears strained to locate the sound. Inside the room? Yes, there, near the bed. The cat? I clapped my hands and the scraping stopped, but after a moment it began again, louder than before.

I stood up, legs and arms stiff, and ran my hand across the bedspread. Tojo was not there. With my fingers I felt my way along the bed to the wall. Again the sound stopped. The black cat must, I thought, be crouched on the floor clawing at the wood paneling.

"Here, Tojo," I whispered. I jumped as the cat slid over my feet. I lifted him, brought him back to the rocker where I sat. His body was warm in my lap. At last a series of short blasts announced the all clear.

I sank back in the chair, relieved. I had never feared

the dark before. Why did I now? Placing the cat on the bed I went to the door and pressed the light switch. Nothing happened. I flipped the switch up and down. The light did not go on. I found the flashlight on the floor beside my chair, opened my door and located the switch in the hall above the empty gun rack. The hall light did not go on. A draft from below chilled my legs and arms. I trembled. Suddenly I felt panic—fear coursed through my body, and only with an effort did I force myself to stand motionless, to think rather than run back to the bedroom and lock myself in.

A fuse has blown, I told myself; nothing more. Where is the fuse box? Probably in the cellar. Aren't they always in the cellar? I searched my memory, but could not recall seeing the box. Holding the light at my side I began to descend the stairs to the hall.

A white image seemed to materialize on the misted glass beside the front door. A face? I gasped, drew back, my hand flying to one side so the flashlight thumped on the wall. The light blinked off. I pressed my body to the paneling, afraid I would lose my balance in the dark and fall. The shape in the window did not move. Not a face, but light reflected from outside on the wet pane. Probably from the streetlight coming on after the all clear.

I pushed the knob on the flashlight. Nothing. I turned the light over in my hand and tightened the front end. The beam of light struck my face, blinding me. I lowered the light to the stairway, waited until I could see and made my way to the cellar door.

A dim light shimmered at the bottom of the cellar stairs, the furnace hissed and the odor of coal hung in the warm air. When I reached the cement of the floor I saw the eerie yellow glow of the fire on the far wall. From somewhere in the dark to my right came the drip, drip, drip of water. The beam of my light glistened on damp whitewashed walls.

I saw a cabinet near the foot of the stairs. The fuse box? I lifted the hook and opened the wooden door. Yes, I faced two rows of round glass fuses.

A yowl—piercing, knife sharp. A crash of breaking glass, a flash of white, a thud on the floor. The light from the furnace flickered on a huddled shape. I swung my flashlight. MacArthur. His white fur was matted and wet. Wet with more than water—with a stain of a color, red, the red of blood. He lay unmoving, lifeless.

I screamed.

# Chapter 12

I ran up the cellar stairs to the hall and swung the beam of the flashlight on the silver-and-black telephone. As I lifted the receiver from the hook I knew with a terrible certainty the line would be dead.

I was wrong—the phone hummed in my ear. "Number please," said the operator's bored voice. What was the number, Jeremy's number? I could not remember.

"I want the Blackstocks, the Jeremy . . . no, the Charles Blackstocks," I said with a rush.

"The number is 319–J," the operator said. "Do you want to write it down?"

"Please get me the number," I pleaded.

"Just a moment, I'll connect you." I counted the rings . . . six, seven, eight. Was no one home?

"Blackstock residence."

"Jeremy?"

"Yes, this is Jeremy. Who's this?"

"Anne, Anne Medford. Brutus, he . . . Come here, now. I want you to see what your dog has done."

"Well . . ." he began. His voice sounded puzzled. "Wait there, I'll be right over."

The phone clicked in my ear. I sat erect in the chair, my breath quick and shallow, all my senses alert. From outside I heard the rain lash the house, while from nearby came the tick, tick of the grandfather clock. I shone my light on the clock's face. Only eight-thirty. I had thought it was much later.

Where was Jeremy? I peered through the clouded pane of the front door, but could see only darkness. Was the dog still roaming loose? With a lurch of fear I remembered the broken window in the cellar. Brutus could get in. I hurried to the cellar door, pushed on the knob until I heard the door click shut.

Steps sounded on the porch followed by the knocker's rapping. I opened the door to see Jeremy's dark silhouette. He had a flashlight in one hand, and water glistened on his black raincoat. "The lights," he said, stepping into the hall and taking off his hat. "You can put on your lights now. Didn't you hear the all clear?"

"They don't work," I told him. My voice quavered; I paused to take a deep breath. "The fuses," I said as I tried to make my tone as calm as I could. "I think a fuse has blown."

He hung his coat on the rack and walked directly to the cellar stairway as though accustomed from long habit to finding his way about the house. His light picked out the fuse box at once. Looking over Jeremy's shoulder I watched him remove the fuses one by one, examine each and screw in replacements from extras on the bottom of the cabinet. A light came on behind me and when I looked up the stairs I saw the glow on the wall of the upstairs hall.

"Odd." Jeremy shook his head. "All your fuses are bad. The new ones seem to work all right, though." He turned from the fuse box to face me.

"Anne," he said, "what was all that on the phone about Brutus? I checked him on my way here and he hasn't— My God!" His eyes followed my mute stare to where the light from the furnace flickered over MacArthur's body huddled on the cellar floor. I felt damp cold air on my legs and, looking above the cat, saw rain blow in through the broken window.

Jeremy shone his light along the ceiling until he found the hanging bulb. He reached up and turned the black knob on the side of the light fixture swaying on its cord; the light came on. He knelt beside the mutilated cat. I glanced at MacArthur's body, then closed my eyes.

"No dog killed this cat," he said. "Look here."

"I can't," I told him. He stood and took my hand, urging me forward.

"Look," he said. I opened my eyes to see his hands pull back the cat's matted fur. "See," Jeremy said, "he was killed by a slashing wound—like a knife makes." The cat's head, almost severed from its body, flopped to one side.

I trembled; my hands clutched at my cheeks, my elbows were pressed tight against my chest. "The window," I whispered. "Could he have cut himself when he came through the glass?"

Jeremy stepped over the cat to look up at the broken slivers of glass that formed a jagged border around the hole. "No blood to speak of on the glass," he said. "See for yourself. Anne, Brutus didn't kill your cat. Why, when I left my house he was inside, not wet or . . ."

"Why must you defend that monster?" I asked. I could hear my voice rise. I fought for control, but could not stop myself. "He attacked me and what did you say, you and your father? No, no, not Brutus—Brutus wouldn't hurt a fly. While I know he tried to kill me and if I hadn't gotten away I'd be lying here on the floor instead of MacArthur. And you, you in your superior way . . ." I began to cry, my words coming between sobs, almost incoherent, my body shaking.

Jeremy gripped my arms near the shoulders. I tried to jerk away, but he followed, holding me. I could feel the heat from the furnace on my back. "Stop, Anne, stop." His voice seemed faint and far away.

"And you wouldn't care if I were dead," I sobbed. He shook me until pain shot up my arms and my head jolted back and forth. The sobs stopped and I looked at him, my eyes wide. His fingers loosened and I buried my face in his chest. I felt his hands on my back. He kissed my forehead. I felt his lips move down my damp cheek and for a moment I clung to him, hands clutching his sweater, feeling his lips search for my mouth.

I stepped back and Jeremy lowered his hands. He stared at me with the light from the fire reflected in his brown eyes. For a moment he didn't move, an expression of distress on his face. Then he looked away.

"Do you have a handkerchief?" I asked, keeping my voice as calm as I could.

He reached into his pocket and handed me one. I dabbed at my face. "Are you all right?" he asked.

"Yes," I said. I was quiet now, exhausted, all emotion drained from me. My fear had abated, the anger at Jeremy was gone. I felt only a sense of surprise at the sudden excitement that had swept over me when he held me in his arms.

"Here," Jeremy said, walking to a pile of wood along one wall, "this will do for now." He propped a board in front of the broken window. He took a shovel from a nail on the side of the coal bin. "Why don't you go upstairs and fix some coffee," he suggested, "while I bury the cat." I nodded. When I reached the top of the stairs I heard the scrape of metal on the cement floor and I shut the door with the image of the mangled body sharp in my mind, the taste of bile in my mouth.

I had the coffee ready when Jeremy returned from outside. He must have forgotten his hat, for his hair was wet, and even after he rubbed his head with a towel and combed his hair the back remained unruly.

"Have some coffee," I said. He sat down and studied me over the rim of his cup as though trying to judge my mood.

"I feel better now," I told him. "I'm sorry I lost my temper. You're right, you know. I once saw a cat that had been killed by a dog and she wasn't cut at all like MacArthur was. But if Brutus didn't, then who or what . . . ?"

Jeremy placed his cup in the saucer and leaned toward me. "Anne," he said, "I don't know. I don't want to frighten you, but you should leave this house. Now, if you can—tomorrow or Monday at the latest." I felt the concern in his low intense voice. Tears gathered in my eyes.

"You and Powers Campbell," I said as I blinked and tried to smile.

"Campbell? The real-estate Campbell?"

"Yes, he stopped by to see me just after I came to Canterbury. He offered me forty thousand dollars for the house."

Jeremy whistled. He pushed back his chair and walked to the window where he stood, hands in pockets, looking out into the night and the storm. He turned to me. "I don't want anything to happen to you, Anne," he said. For an instant, looking at Jeremy, I thought of my father, though they looked nothing alike. "Will you, Anne?"

"Move? Let me think about it," I said. Why should I leave? I asked myself. Why do they all want me to go? A sudden suspicion came into my mind. "Do you know something I don't?" I asked him. "Something you're not telling me?"

Jeremy frowned and once more stared out the window. I looked at the reflection on the black surface—the kitchen, me sitting at the table, Jeremy. I tried to read his expression, but his breath misted the glass. "I don't think so," he said. He ran his hand over his hair. "I've never liked this house—all the time I've lived next door. I've told you that. There's a wrongness here, a feeling of malevolence I can't explain."

"You'll feel different when I finish remodeling," I said. I rinsed the coffee cups in the sink.

"Could I look through the house?" he asked. "Would you mind?"

"No, not at all. But what can you hope to find?"

"Whatever makes this relic of the 1850s worth forty thousand dollars to someone," he said.

He began in the cellar. I waited at the top of the stairs with the clock loud in my ears. He was in the basement a long time and when he came back to the hall I saw a dark smear on his face and his hands were black. After he washed in the kitchen he made a cursory inspection of Mrs. Allison's rooms. He was done in a few minutes.

The second floor interested Jeremy more. He walked from room to room, stopping to stare at windows, walls, ceilings, to poke into closets. The walls of the empty bedrooms were all papered with the same design—roses climbing a trellis—but in different colors. When Jeremy entered my bedroom he glanced around as though ill at ease.

"You've done a lot of work," he said when he came back into the hall, shutting the door behind him.

"And I've a great deal more to do."

"What's this?" He knelt in front of the rifle-high gun rack. Metal bars crossed its front—bars hinged on one end and padlocked on the other.

"I can't find the keys," I told him.

He shrugged, walked to the banister and looked down over the front hall. I stood behind him. Jeremy seemed to belong here, I thought, and not just because he was familiar with the house. When I was alone, the gloominess, the high ceilings and the ornate carvings intimidated me. Jeremy, on the other hand, with his tall good looks, his easy confidence, dominated and subdued the house.

"The attic?" he asked. He had turned to find me staring at him. His eyes held mine.

"What?" I asked, confused. "Oh, yes, I'll show you." As I led the way up the stairs he reached above our heads to pull the light cord. Rain drummed on the roof; with a swoosh the wind changed and the noise slackened for a few moments, only to return more insistent than before.

Jeremy explored the dusty interiors of trunks and wardrobes. He knelt to shine his light into the recesses where the roof met the floor. I watched him for a time; then I walked beyond one of the great brick chimneys to a cleared space on the far side. The light was dim in the chimney's shadow, but I could see a massive table piled high with magazines; chairs alternately right side up and upside down; and a cloth-covered cabinet I had not noticed before.

A phonograph. I folded the cloth, lifted the top and found the needle still in place. I cranked the handle on the side and watched, with surprise, as the turntable began to rotate. I knelt in front of the cabinet and found a rack built into the bottom between the legs. I removed a record—"Among My Souvenirs"—slid off the paper jacket, placed the record on the turntable and lowered the needle onto it.

The slow, brassy music of a dance band swelled above the sounds of the storm. I hummed to myself; then, feeling eyes on me, I looked around to see Jeremy leaning against the chimney, looking at me. I brushed a stray lock of hair from my eyes. Jeremy smiled, walked to me. I slid into his arms and we danced, the music a sad and melancholy lament for a lost love. The rain and the wind closed us in so we were apart from the rest of the world, secure in the cavelike attic, alone, just he and I.

The record groaned to a halt—I hadn't wound the phonograph enough. I looked into Jeremy's dark face and closed my eyes. He kissed me, his lips warm, and I felt his body against mine. Nothing existed for me but Jeremy—there was no wind, no rain, the attic faded like a dissolving scene in a movie. Only Jeremy, tall, commanding, his firm hands on my back drawing me to him. I wanted the kiss to last forever, wanted to lose myself in him. Never before had I felt as I did now. Oh, yes, yes, yes, a voice within me whispered and, my excitement rising, I moved my lips on his, returned his kiss. He paused, then drew me even closer within his arms. I put my hand to the back of his neck; I felt his hair soft under my fingers.

He stepped away, held me from him—and once more I saw the look of pain on his face. He shook his head. "No, I can't," he said. His voice was husky, anguished. "I'm sorry, I wish, I wish—you don't know. . . ." The words trailed off. He released me and his feet thudded away across the attic floor. I wanted to call to him, tell him to come back, but I did not.

"Please, Anne," he said, looking at me from the head of the stairs, "leave this house before it's too late." I heard his footsteps on the stairs. After a minute the front door opened and closed and he was gone.

I took the record from the turntable and replaced

it in the rack. Passing the chimney, I ran my fingertips along the rough surface of the bricks. The attic seemed so huge and empty. I looked at my reflection in the window, saw a loose strand of hair on my forehead, felt the tears on my cheeks. A gust of wind drove rain against the window and rivulets of water ran down the pane. I hugged my arms about myself and cried.

# Chapter 13

I awakened several times to hear the hard, steady beat of the rain on the sides of the house. Then, in the waning hours of the night—the time just before dawn when, my father had said, the very sick are most apt to die—I dreamed.

I rode in a carriage drawn by four white horses along a cobbled street to an open gate flanked by black, up-thrusting pillars. The driveway curved between flaming torches to a great house aglow with lights and I recognized my house at Canterbury—not as it was today, but as it must have been years before: resplendent and alive.

The coachman handed me from the carriage and a red-coated doorman hurried forward to lead me to the porch. As I entered the ballroom I felt the eyes of men and women on me, felt them stare at my long white dress and the diamond tiara on my head. On the far side of the room stood a tall man surrounded by women and I recognized Jeremy—yet at the same time I knew he was John Lorch. He looked up, smiled, nodded apologies to the others and walked across the room toward me. In the hush I could hear his footsteps click on the parquet dance floor. I was expectant, yet afraid. The orchestra, as though on signal, began a waltz and he held his arms out to me and we danced.

Whispers came from the circle of spectators who watched us: "Who is she?" "Anne Medford." "She's lovely." "He chose Anne Medford." The voices were envious, but at the same time I sensed a relief, an end to waiting, to not knowing.

When the music stopped Jeremy kept my hand and escorted me to a double door carved with nymphs and satyrs. Two men leaped forward to open the door. I stopped when a wave of heat flowed from within; I peered into the blackness to see a fire pulse with tongues of red-and-orange flame. Beside the fire a man waited, huge and muscular, naked to the waist, sweat gleaming on his body. Jeremy was gone, the ballroom was gone, and I was in a dark underground chamber; yet I felt the eyes of the guests still on me. The man smiled, motioned me to come to him. I shook my head and saw the smile contort into a leer. He strode toward me and I turned to run but I could not. I screamed.

I sat up in bed, shivering in the cold room, the terror still coursing through me. My hands cupped my face and I sobbed, but no tears came. Dazed, I tried to separate dream from reality. I looked about me and saw the outline of the nightstand, the dresser, the rectangles of the windows. I was awake. Rain beat on the house. Trembling, I turned on the light and sat waiting for the dawn. Later I must have dozed, for I woke to a buzzing in my ears. The telephone—the telephone was ringing. I swung both feet to the bare floor and hurried to the door in the muted light of early morning. When I reached the hall the ringing stopped. Jeremy? I returned to the bedroom, hugging myself for warmth.

The unchanging roses, one above the other, faced me from the wall behind my bed. Not today, I thought. I didn't want to scrape wallpaper today—I was too tired from my interrupted sleep. I felt twinges in my arms and legs when I moved. Still, I thought, I should.

I brought my juice, toast and coffee to the bedroom. Before I ate I walked to the windows where I pulled aside the drapes. A metallic rain fell from heavy clouds.

Trees leaned before the wind coming off the river. I looked over to the Blackstock house, squat and dreary in the storm; I searched for some sign of life, hoped for a glimpse of Jeremy, but saw no one.

Absently I spread jam on my toast. He's no different from any other man, I told myself. Not as good-looking as Karl, surely, nor as thoughtful. Karl would do anything in the world for me. I went to the nightstand and held his picture in both my hands. "With All My Love." When Karl loved a women he was responsive to her every wish. She's lucky, my friends had thought when they saw me with Karl.

And Don—friendly, bumbling Don. He's the kind of person I could be comfortable with, I thought, not only today and tomorrow, but next year and the year after as well. The better I knew him the more I liked Don. True, I'd get impatient with him at times, insist he finish writing his book, and with me to push him a bit, he would. I could hear the other members of the faculty. "Aren't Don and Anne a lovely couple?" they'd ask one another.

Jeremy, of course, was impossible. I could still feel the sting of tears from the night before when he had left me alone in the attic. I'd made a fool of myself. After I'd practically thrown myself at him he'd held me away. What had he said? He was sorry? *Sorry.* Wait until the next time he asked me for a date. Perhaps to go dancing—he enjoyed dancing. Or he'd want me to go to dinner and a show.

"I'm sorry," I'd say, "I'm sorry, Jeremy, you don't know how sorry I am, but I can't possibly this week. The PTA meets Thursday night and on Friday Don Nevins and I chaperone the first dance of the year. Who's Don Nevins? He's the English teacher at school who used to be a football star on one of the big college teams. Saturday? Oh, the faculty tea at the YWCA is on Saturday." I could say all this and only have to invent the dance and the tea.

"How would Tuesday the week after next at seven-thirty be?" I'd ask him. "Of course I'll have to be home by ten because the first report card period ends the next day and I have to finish averaging grades.

"You don't think grading should take long? You obviously don't understand what's involved. That's right, though, I'd forgotten you only went two years to college." Then Jeremy would scowl and he'd slam the door on his way out and I'd never be bothered by him again.

If I relented—if he was contrite and I wanted to show I didn't hold a grudge—if he did take me out I supposed I'd wear the yellow silk. I hadn't worn the yellow dress in Canterbury. Was the neckline too low? Of course, it would never do at a school event, but to go dancing or to dinner at a hotel the yellow silk would be fine. Yes, I'd definitely wear the yellow silk.

I hoped there'd be a moon. Isn't the weather usually clear after a storm? Jeremy had said moonlight became me the night we went dancing; even asked the band to play the song. And candlelight, dinner by candlelight would be perfect. Afterwards, when we came home, would he kiss me good night? Of course he would. He had kissed me once already, there was no reason he wouldn't again.

I hummed the song I'd played on the phonograph in the attic, "Among My Souvenirs;" the words made me sad but joyous at the same time. Yes, I thought, he'd kiss me. I remembered his arms around me, his lips on mine, and I shivered. Never had I known such a complete awareness of myself and of the moment—nothing else had mattered, neither the past nor the future. It had been a feeling that no one, ever, can adequately describe.

While I washed the breakfast dishes I sang under my breath. The words of popular songs, however trite and banal, seemed to have new meaning. I pictured Jeremy—his greying hair, his deep brown eyes, the mouth ready to turn up to smile or down into a frown.

The phone rang. Wiping my hands as I went, I walked quickly to the stairs and down to the lower hall. Make it be Jeremy, I thought. I picked the receiver from the hook after the third ring.

"Hi, Don Nevins here. How are you?"

"I'm fine, Don," I said. I was annoyed at myself for feeling so disappointed.

"I called earlier."

"Oh," I said. "I wondered who that was before. I reached the phone too late."

"Would you like to go to the show tonight? I hear the picture at the village theater is real good."

"Tonight?" I hesitated. Should I tell him I had other plans, was sorry, I'd be glad to go another time—hoping Jeremy would call later? Why should I spend the day waiting for Jeremy? No, I told myself, I'd show Jeremy I wasn't at his beck and call. "Why, yes, Don," I said, "tonight would be fine. What time?"

"I'll be by at quarter till seven. Have your galoshes ready—it's raining cats and dogs."

"Yes," I said, "I know."

After I put the phone down I walked from empty room to empty room. Yesterday, with Jeremy, this house had seemed to come alive, while today all I could hear was the echo of my footsteps in the cryptlike silence. I sighed. Why try to fool yourself, Anne? Admit what's happened. I know, I answered, the symptoms are all there. A high-school freshman could make the diagnosis.

I was in love with Jeremy Blackstock.

The cold, sullen day dragged on. Distracted and bemused, I worked fitfully, washed clothes, laid socks and underclothes on radiators to dry, ironed, worked the crossword in last night's paper, finished the jigsaw puzzle, tried to read—but gave up when I found I had finished only one page after fifteen minutes. I kept remembering how Jeremy had looked at me, what he had said, how I had felt when he held me in his arms.

Mrs. Allison called around two. "I'm staying over another week," she said. "I called you, Anne, because I didn't want you to worry. My sister is taking me shopping in the city next week and we're going to a play. The storm didn't do any damage, did it? You don't mind looking after MacArthur and Tojo for a week, do you?"

Should I tell Mrs. Allison about MacArthur? I shuddered, picturing his lifeless body. I thought of Mrs. Allison's lonely life here in Canterbury and the son she had refused to admit was dead. Why upset her when she was enjoying herself? MacArthur, buried in the rain-soaked earth, was beyond help. "Everything's all right," I said. "Have a good time."

When the rain let up around six I looked from the window hoping to see the sun, and noticed a movement in the Blackstocks' yard. I stood behind the curtain and saw a man beneath the pines in a black raincoat and a dark hat; he was almost invisible in the early twilight. He waited stolidly, as though unaware of the light though steady rain; his eyes never left the front of my house.

Suddenly he straightened and walked toward the front gate. I saw another man, shorter, stockier, come from the street and open the gate. I recognized Charles Blackstock. Jeremy, for the watcher had been Jeremy, talked to his father and then the two men went up the path to the house. When they reached the porch the clouds seemed to close in and the rain came down hard once more. As I changed clothes for my date with Don I was uneasy, troubled. How long had Jeremy stood in the shadows of the pines? Why had he been watching the house?

Don was late. "One of my headlights," he explained. "Usually goes on if I get out and hit it, but not tonight, not at first anyway." He paused. "You look awfully nice," he said. I wore a tailored blue suit.

"Thank you," I told him. He helped me into my raincoat and held an umbrella for me as we walked to his car. We got to our seats in the theater just as the newsreel ended. When my eyes became accustomed to the dark I noticed the back of a man's head three rows in front of us. He looked familiar. Was it Jeremy? When I sat up straight and leaned to my right to get a better view I found a woman's head in the way. I leaned to my left.

"Can you see?" Don asked.

"Yes, just stretching," I whispered. I settled back.

No, the man wasn't Jeremy—he wasn't tall enough to be Jeremy.

I couldn't get interested in the movie. It was an old Will Rogers picture, and I liked Will Rogers. The story was about a race horse that only ran well in the mud. Will Rogers was a rainmaker who sent dynamite aloft in balloons so the explosion would bring rain. During the big race, the balloon caught on a high tank, but just when the race seemed lost the dynamite went off, the tank burst, water flooded the track, and the horse won.

After the show we walked a half block to Lawrence's Drug Store. As I sat in a booth sipping a soda through a straw I felt like a young girl again; it was a safe, comfortable feeling. Two of my students walked by. "Hi, Miss Medford," they said, sounding surprised to see me. I half listened as Don told me about an essay contest one of his classes was holding in connection with the annual exhibit. Don, I knew, worked hard at being a good teacher.

He drove me home and, as he said good night, he held my hand for a moment. Yes, I thought while I watched his car go down the drive, Don was easy to like. He reminded me of someone. My father? They don't look alike, I thought, they don't act alike. Yet there was something about Don, the way he talked or the way he smiled, that brought back a memory of my father.

Don stopped his car before he reached the street, got out and gave his right headlight a sharp blow with his fist. The light snapped on. Don saw me standing on the porch, waved and drove off.

Rain was still falling during my trigonometry class early Monday morning. When I looked out a half hour later, while I drew problems on the blackboard in preparation for plane geometry, I found the rain had stopped and blue sky showed above the river. The storm was over.

I went home after school, changed and walked on rain-darkened sidewalks to the village. A boy, riding past on a bicycle, raised his legs high above the pedals to coast through a puddle. The bus from Newburgh pulled up in front of Santoro's and the driver carried a bundle of newspapers to three waiting boys. One of the boys squatted and cut the cord and they began counting and thrusting papers into their cloth carryingbags. Behind them Mark Santoro used a long metal rod to unroll the awning over the front of his store. He jumped back as rainwater, trapped in the folds of the awning, splashed to the sidewalk.

I turned down River Street and entered the office of the weekly paper, the *Canterbury Local*. A short, balding man said yes, they did keep copies of their old newspapers and showed me to a back room where shelflike compartments lined the lower portion of one wall, each with a date printed above: 1920, 1921, 1922, year by year to 1944. The man left me by myself, as I had hoped he would. I soon found what I was looking for in the dusty papers from the winter of 1934:

BLACKSTOCK LEADS CHS TIGERS PAST MONROE, 59–45
BLACKSTOCK SCORES 26 IN CHS UPSET WIN

I recognized his picture without reading the caption—a tall boy with black hair flying as he leaped high, a basketball arching from his fingertips. I turned the pages and stopped when I saw another headline, large and black, across the top of the page:

MILL STRIKE ENDS

I read the article, surprised. I hadn't realized his mother had left the same year. For Jeremy, a year of success and tragedy. I was troubled and puzzled as I returned the papers to the shelf.

I was thinking too much of Jeremy, I decided. My teaching suffered because I was distracted—in a pleasant daze. This can't go on, I told myself. I wanted something to happen—anything would be better than waiting and wondering.

My wish came true all too soon. The beginning, although I didn't realize it at the time, came with the next meeting of the math club.

Carroll Johnson raised his hand and I nodded to him. "I was thinking," he said, "in this high school the biggest turnout of students comes when they're trying out for one of the teams like basketball or baseball. Why can't we do the same with mathematics? Couldn't we have a Canterbury mathematics team? We could challenge other schools like Monroe, Beacon, or even Newburgh."

No one said a word. The other two boys stared straight ahead without expression. Jack Gerken spoke first. "We could have different events," he said slowly. "Some for speed, others using longer, harder problems."

"There'd be two divisions," Don Novak said, "one for freshmen and sophomores, the other for juniors and seniors."

"We might have a game," Carroll said, "where we were given a problem and had to go to the blackboard and explain our answer just using a piece of chalk to show the solution."

"A chalk-talk contest," I said. I felt excited. Carroll's idea was a good one; it had all sorts of possibilities. Why hadn't I thought of it?

"Probably Merritt Peck would want to be on the team," Jack said. "He's good at speaking off the cuff."

"And maybe Lois Neal and Mildred O'Brien," Carroll added.

After they left the room, still making plans, I stood by my second-floor window, the heat from the radiator warm on my legs, and watched students leaving the school grounds. Three boys ran across the street laughing and shouting, an older boy and girl strolled hand in hand on the sidewalk, and two grade-school pupils played marbles next to the building directly beneath me. I smiled, feeling a glow of pleasure when I thought of Carroll's suggestion. I'd call the Monroe High School math teacher tomorrow.

I turned back to the room and wrote "Please Save" under the triangles on the board. Scalene, equilateral, isosceles triangles—no sides the same, all sides the same, two the same. I gasped. Why hadn't I noticed before? Now I knew what seemed wrong about my house. I would have to check, of course, but I had no doubt I was right. That one wall, the paneled wall in my bedroom, was not the same. What did it mean?

# Chapter 14

Don Nevins opened my classroom door and looked in. "Ready to go?" he asked. For the past week he had made a habit of stopping after school to walk with me as far as the village. "I have to go to Santoro's to pick up my paper," he said. Once or twice I'd considered discouraging him, but I liked his company—no, more than that, I liked *him,* and I saw no harm in going around with him as long as he expected only friendship. Don gave no indication of wanting more.

"Just a minute," I told him. I walked next door to the lounge and put on my grey coat with the fox-fur collar.

"We began *A Tale of Two Cities* today,' Don said when I joined him in the hall. "I always look forward to reading Dickens."

"'It is a far, far better thing I do than I have ever done,' " I quoted.

"Seems corny now," Don said, smiling, "yet every time I read that passage I get a feeling of—well, romance is the best word, I guess. Dickens has a way with him. And those marvelous names he gave his characters—Pecksniff, Martin Chuzzlewit, Ebenezer Scrooge."

"I always liked Uriah Heep," I said. "I could picture him just from his name."

As we strolled along the side of the school I could hear boys' shouts and the thud of soccer balls from the playground. The air had turned cold after the storm—most mornings I woke to lawns white with frost—and the trees beyond the soccer fields reached bare limbs to the sky. An occasional leaf still clung to a black branch as if refusing to acknowledge the coming of winter, but there was no question the storm had signaled the end of one season and the beginning of another.

Don and I stood on an embankment overlooking the playing field. Two rows of boys in orange-and-black sweatshirts, one row on each side of the field, sent soccer balls soaring back and forth between them. In front of the white posts of the goal three boys took turns making penalty kicks at the goalie, who leaped, arms outflung, to block the hard-driven balls. To our right girls in white caps and shorts played tennis. Charley, the girls' gym teacher, saw us, waved, and we waved back. I was beginning to feel this was really my school. I thought that I had been more than just accepted—I felt needed.

"I typed two pages of my book over the weekend," Don said, "and I'm going back to change some of the chapters I wrote before. My point of view won't be as cynical or as negative. I'm trying to make the story more true-to-life, with what's good about education as well as all that's wrong."

"I still want to read the novel when you're done," I said.

"You will, Anne," he promised. Don dislodged a stone with his toe and lofted it down the bank. "After all, you're responsible for my working on the book again. You're the first person who seemed interested in what I was doing."

"I am interested, Don," I told him. We turned from the field and began to walk toward the street. Although the last three days had been sunny the ground was still muddy, and I saw puddles on the dirt road leading from the playground.

We passed the post office, Lawrence's Drug Store, the grocery store, at ease with one another; we had no need for words. Passing the large glass window of the meat market, I saw Mr. Clark, the butcher, look up from his chopping block, recognize me and nod. I smiled at him. Still elated about the math club, I described to Don Carroll's idea of a math team to compete with other schools.

Don nodded. "Carroll's got a good head on his shoulders," he said.

Two small boys ran by us, laughing, and one snatched the other's hat and threw it across a puddle into the meat-market parking lot. The boy retrieved his hat, but when he ran through the mud one of his shoes, laces hanging, caught in the goo and came off. He hopped back on one foot, pushed his other into the shoe and jumped to the sidewalk. The boy, who was probably one of Mrs. Calyer's kindergarten pupils, knelt a short distance in front of us, his curly black hair falling over his forehead. I saw his friend duck into the outer lobby of a movie theater in the next block.

The boy fumbled as he tried to tie the laces of his shoe. "Here, let me help," I said. He looked up, shy and startled, but then he smiled. I squatted beside him and he put his small hands on my shoulder. When I saw a tear glisten in his eye I wanted to put my arms around him and hold him close. I felt an ache, a longing. I sighed and pulled his laces tight and made a bow.

"Thanks," he mumbled and ran on; then he stopped and smiled back at me. The other boy dashed from the lobby. "Hey, wait for me," the black-haired boy called. They ran around a corner and disappeared behind the telephone-company building.

I stood up to find Don's light-brown eyes watching me. "I brought you a present," he said. He reached into the pocket of his overcoat and handed me a chrysanthemum, a perfect small flower, gold and brown, the colors of autumn. I held the flower in my hand, feeling tears come to my eyes.

"Mums are my favorite flowers," I said. I started to put the stem in my buttonhole.

"Wait, let me," Don said. With a straight pin he fastened the flower to the top of my coat. He walked beside me, his boyish face serious and composed, his eyes on me; finally I looked away, flustered. Had I been wrong when I thought Don would be satisfied with friendship?

We reached the five corners. "I'll see you at PTA tonight," I said, trying to make my voice matter-of-fact.

"Swell. This year I actually look forward to PTA

meetings." He didn't go into Santoro's, but stood on the sidewalk; I knew he was watching me walk away. I was surprised and flattered, yet I felt guilty as well. How do you keep a man for a friend? I wondered. I liked Don and didn't want to hurt him, and now I knew I could. Maybe I should be busy the next time he calls, I thought.

At home I put on slacks, a blouse and my old rubber-soled saddle shoes. I'll use yesterday's leftovers, I decided, to make a hot beef sandwich for supper. First the bedroom—I must check to see if I was right.

When I'd seen the isosceles triangle on the blackboard with its two sides the same, I'd remembered I had never seen another wall in any of the upstairs rooms paneled with wood the way the section of the wall behind my bed was paneled. Shouldn't the other side be the same? Every wall of the other rooms was papered with the same roses climbing the same trellises. The builder could have papered over a wood wall, but that, I thought, was unlikely.

I went into the hall. Across from my room I had left the key in the attic door, for that door, like the one to my bedroom, refused to close unless it was locked. I walked slowly toward the back of the house. Only one other door opened off the hall on the same side as my room, a door leading to a small bedroom. I stepped inside. As I had remembered, the room extended to only about half the depth of my room. The paneled section of the wall would be beyond.

Back in the hall I turned left into a narrow, dark corridor and saw the feeble light from a window at the far end. When I reached the window I looked into the dusk at the lights in the Blackstock house. The bushes in the yards were black and somber and the river at the bottom of the slope was hidden under a grey mist. I shivered involuntarily when I saw Brutus ambling along the Blackstock side of the fence. I turned the round knob on the radiator under the window and listened to the knock of steam rising in the pipes.

To my right stairs led down to the kitchen. I opened

the door to the bedroom across from the stairs and went into a small square room; its two windows faced the Blackstocks'. I stepped to the side of the doorway and switched on the lights to reveal dust covers still shrouding a bed, desk and chest of drawers. The closet was located, oddly, on the hall side of the room. On the wall across from me, the wall on the other side of the wood paneling in my bedroom, green roses climbed a brown trellis. I ran my fingers over the surface of the wall, tapped with my knuckles and heard the solid sound of plaster.

Could the wall be plaster on this side, wood on the other? Possibly, yet I knew the paneling had not seemed to be a veneer, a covering, but definitely part of the wall itself. I stood in the center of the room with hands on hips. Was there a space between the two rooms? How could I be sure?

The tape measure. I had returned the tape to the tool chest in the cellar when I finished measuring the outside of the house. I walked hurriedly to the hall, down the front stairs and into the cellar. At the bottom of the cellar steps I averted my eyes from the dark stain on the cement floor that, despite my scrubbing, had refused to come off. I frowned and clenched my fists as I remembered how MacArthur's severed head had flopped to one side.

The tape measure was on top of a clutter of files, saws, pliers, hammers and assorted cardboard boxes of screws and nails. Although the house was now dark I had come to know its mazelike turnings, and I made my way back to the first floor hall without switching on the light.

Tojo cried from the front porch so I stopped to open the door. Alongside the porch my car, which I planned to drive to the PTA meeting, sat in the shadows. Tojo walked stiff-legged to the cellar door where he sniffed, then mewed plaintively—as though he mourned MacArthur. When the white cat had been alive, Tojo had ignored him, but now that MacArthur was dead he seemed disconsolate. I knelt and stroked him beneath his chin, ran my fingers along his back until he purred. The cat followed me up the stairs.

Upstairs, I measured the distance one end of the hall to the other. Thirty-five feet. The distance from the paneled wall of my bedroom to the wall opposite plus the distance from the other side of the paneled wall to the door of the small square back bedroom should also be about thirty-five feet. In my bedroom I ran the tape along the floor from door to wall. Sixteen feet. Going into the back bedroom, I hooked the end of the tape on the doorframe and unrolled the metal to the wall. I read the number on the tape and drew in my breath.

Twelve feet. A difference of seven feet, an unaccounted-for seven feet. Had I made a mistake? I took the measurements again. They were the same. Between my room and the back bedroom was a space seven feet wide and some twelve feet long.

I opened the door from my bedroom to the balcony and walked along the side of the house to where the balcony ended just beyond the window at the end of the narrow rear corridor. Other than that window and the two windows of the small bedroom I found no opening in the weathered wood clapboards.

All at once I realized I was hungry, for I had eaten only cottage cheese for lunch. As I ate my hot beef sandwich, keyed up by my discovery and at the same time wary and unsure of the meaning of what I had found, I tried to picture the room behind the wall. Had it been built almost a hundred years ago, part of the original plan for the house? Had the room once had an entrance and, if so, where? Or could there be another explanation? Perhaps no room existed after all. The chimneys—I hadn't thought of the chimneys, although I knew at least six of them led from either the cellar or the first floor to the roof. No, the space was too large for a chimney or even a combination of chimneys.

After I washed the dishes I looked at the clock on the bureau. Ten after six. I still had time before I had to change clothes for the meeting. The phone rang. The hall was black with night and I turned on the lights of the chandelier from the top of the stairs.

"Hello," I said.

"This is Jeremy." I heard my breath quicken so I put my hand over the cone-shaped mouthpiece. "Anne, are you there?" he asked.

"Yes, how are you, Jeremy?" With an effort I kept my voice controlled and impersonal.

"Good," he answered. "I've been busy all week. Say, I have to drive over to Middletown after supper to deliver some work. How about coming with me? The business will only take a few minutes."

I was about to say yes when I remembered the meeting. I grimaced. "I'd love to," I said, "but we've got a PTA meeting tonight and I have to say a few words about this year's math program. All the teachers are telling what their students will be doing. It's sort of an orientation for the parents."

"I understand," Jeremy said. "I'm sorry you can't go. Just a spur-of-the-minute idea, anyway." I couldn't tell if he sounded disappointed. "I see you haven't taken my advice," he said.

"Your advice? Oh, you mean about moving. No, I'm not going to. I've decided to stay. You can't get rid of me that easily," I added in a teasing voice.

There was a pause. Evidently Jeremy found my remark as lacking in humor as I did myself. "How about Saturday afternoon?" he asked with one of his abrupt changes in subject. "I could show you some of Canterbury you might not have seen yet."

"Wonderful," I said, hoping he didn't hear my elation. "I've been so busy with school and the house and all, I've hardly explored any of the village."

Should I tell him about the sealed room, or rather what I suspected to be a sealed room? No, I thought, I'll wait and surprise him. I half admitted to myself another reason for not mentioning the room, an unsureness that kept me silent. For an instant I pictured Jeremy as I had first seen him, standing behind Brutus at the fence; then I pictured Brutus loping behind his master toward the Blackstock house. I shivered.

"Around one o'clock Saturday," he said. "I'll see you then." Less than two days from now, I thought after I hung up. I sat beside the telephone staring at light reflected from the glass panel on the front door. I imagined Jeremy leading me into a secluded glen where a stream bubbled below us and rocky banks rose high on both sides. After he'd spread a blanket on top of a flat rock he'd hold his hand out to me, and when I'd reached the top he'd pull me to him and his arms would enfold me. I'd lift my face to his. . . .

I blinked away the daydream. Once more I saw the glow of the hall chandelier on the glass pane. I still have time, I thought, to see what I can discover about the room behind the paneling. I opened the door to the cellar and pressed the light switch, for I had found I could turn the knob of the hanging cellar light to "on" and then control the light from the top of the stairs. I didn't want to return to the basement room, but I had no choice.

Once more I avoided the bloodstain on the floor as I crossed to the tool box. After rummaging through the hammers, wrenches and drills, I found a large screw-driver—not the ordinary kind, but one over a foot long with a black wood handle and a thick blade. It was more like a chisel than a screwdriver. As an afterthought I also took one of the hammers.

Back in my room I examined the wall. At the corner, a narrow strip of dark wood went from baseboard to ceiling to cover the joining of the plaster and wood. I inserted the screwdriver, but the fit was so snug the blade would not penetrate until I pounded on the handle with the hammer. The wood strip bulged where the blade forced it up. Using the screwdriver as a lever I pushed the handle toward the wall and saw the strip spring loose. I slid the blade of the screwdriver down toward the floor until, with a sharp crack, the bottom of the board came free. Standing on a chair I levered the top loose and the piece of wood clattered to the floor.

Underneath I found that the paneling, which consisted of boards of various widths going from floor to ceiling, came to within an inch of the wall perpendicular to it. The last board was nailed to a heavy vertical timber. The edge of the plaster next to the timber was smooth, as though at one time this had not been a corner—as if the room had once formed an L with the sealed room the bottom arm of the letter.

The cat, who had watched me from the bed, leaped past onto the floor. When he sniffed at the heavy timber his back arched, his hair bristled. He hissed, the sound like a quick intake of breath. "It's all right, Tojo," I said while I rubbed him beneath the ears and under the chin. He looked doubtful, but let me lift him back onto the bed.

I turned to the wall. Using both hammer and screwdriver I pried loose the edge of the first board. Besides being nailed to the timber, the board was held in place by narrow strips of wood near the ceiling and the baseboard, so I removed them as well. When the board sprang free I grasped the sides in both hands, backed away and let the board drop to the floor.

I pressed my face to the narrow slit and peered into the darkness of the room.

# Chapter 15

A heavy, musty odor came from the black interior, the smell of stale air and dampness. There was also another scent that I could not identify. The gap was less than a foot wide, too narrow for me to crawl through, so I brought the flashlight from the dresser and shone the light into the opening. Inside I saw a chest of drawers on the opposite side of the small room and, although it was shrouded by a grey coat of dust, I recognized the mahogany pattern of my bedroom furniture. I could see two shapes on top of the chest that looked like a book and a jewelry box.

I swung the light to the right along the side wall,

the house's outer wall, but found nothing except cobweb streamers and a claw-legged radiator. The floor was covered by a worn, dust-coated rug. To the left I saw the foot of a bed whose head must have been against the wall behind my bed, but the angle was too great for me to see more than part of the sideboard and the foot.

I felt the hair rise on the back of my neck. The bed was of the same dark mahogany design. This was the missing bed for which I searched the morning after my arrival in Canterbury! Why had the metal bed been substituted in the large bedroom while the matching one was left here?

Placing the flashlight on the floor behind me I pried at the next section of wood paneling. The board snapped loose with a report like the shot of a rifle. Startled, I looked behind me as though I expected someone to have heard. I saw only Tojo staring solemnly from the bed. The opening was now wide enough that I could enter the room so long hidden from view.

I hesitated, glancing at the clock on my bureau. I should get ready for the meeting, I thought. Yet I knew this was an excuse and not the real reason for my reluctance. I had begun my exploration with the sense of expectancy an adventurer must feel when he searches for buried treasure. I did not know what I might find in the room, but I no longer expected treasure. Instead I recalled old tales heard when I was a child, tales of being imprisoned alive behind brick walls, and I shuddered. I remembered my drive to Canterbury when I had been alone in my car on the rainswept mountainside, felt the aloneness I had known then.

Should I wait until I saw Don at the meeting and ask him to explore the room with me? No, I told myself. What have I to fear from the past? Not only the past, but someone else's past, not mine.

With the flashlight in my hand I stooped under a crossbeam to enter the dark room, choking and coughing as my movements raised a swirl of dust. I blinked, my eyes smarting. I could see only motes of dust spinning in the beam of light; I waited, and gradually the air cleared and I swung the light across the chest of drawers and along the far wall. Trailers of cobwebs everywhere. I felt a tingle run along my spine as I saw the red-velvet wallpaper.

Clothes were folded neatly on a chair at the foot of the bed, and near the chair on a small table sat a woman's hat, once black but now grey. Then the bed itself, the mahogany footboard carved in ornate designs, a heavy dust-laden quilt, lumped and untidy, and . . .

I screamed. The flashlight fell from my hand, going out as it thudded to the floor. Bile rose in my throat to my mouth and I gagged, the foul taste choking me. I ducked back under the beam, striking my head in my panic, and staggered into the large room where I fell full-length on the bed, my hand to my mouth as I gasped for air. My head throbbed. I forced myself to think, wildly, irrelevantly, of Jeremy, Carroll Johnson, the school, Don; my mind shifting here, there, anyplace other than to the horror I had left behind in the dust-choked room.

Trembling, I pulled the blanket from the foot of the bed up to my chin, wrapped myself cocoonlike into the covering, buried my head under the pillow, tried to make my mind blank. No use, for the scene had seared itself into my consciousness—it would leave a brand I could never remove.

I had seen two forms beneath the quilt. A stain, no, several stains marred its variegated design. Black holes punctured the fabric. Two pillows, each indented, lay at the head of the double bed, and on the pillows rested the horror. The horrors, for there were two. The eyes were the worst—not the eyes, the lack of eyes, the gaping holes, the black stare of sockets where eyes should be. And the hair, the woman's short and black, the man's blond. The hair had looked incongruous, as though it had lived on after the bodies had died.

Again I felt nausea rise within me and I held my hand over my mouth, gagging. Curling myself on the bed, knees up, I stared unseeing at the windows and the night. I don't know how long I lay rigid on the bed, without thought, without strength. Finally the cat leaped up beside me and I felt his nose on my hair and his soft fur against my face. I stroked him until he purred and I lay with my hand kneading his warm body. At last I sat up, then stood, eyes averted from the gap in the wall. I proceeded out of the room, my hand grasping first the foot of the bed, then the rocker, then the doorframe.

In the bathroom I washed my face and hands with cold water. My face in the mirror was pale, my eyes bloodshot, and for an instant I saw those other eyes, empty and lifeless, and I covered my face with my hands and turned away.

With my arms folded across my chest I walked into the upper hall, where I paced from the front past the attic's locked door, the gun rack, the other bedroom doors, to the back corridor. I returned the length of the long gloomy hall, feeling dizzy, seeing spots before my eyes. I rested on the railing over the downstairs hall, but the height sickened me and I leaned back against the wall.

John Lorch had been my first thought when I discovered the secret of the sealed room. I recalled what I knew of him—the velvet wallpaper, his violent death, his murderer confined to a hospital for the criminally insane. I had assumed the two bodies were from the time when John Lorch had lived in this house, more than thirty years before.

Now my mind began to cover over the raw wound of my discovery as earth covers the graves of the dead, and I could think of something other than that gruesome discovery. I began to doubt whether John Lorch was involved at all. Hadn't the house been searched after his murder? I was sure Charles Blackstock had told me it had. But if the bodies were not connected with John Lorch, where had they come from?

I remembered the clothes on the chair. I pursed my lips as I attempted to picture them in my mind—a short black dress, underclothes and a cloche hat on a table, a hat such as women had worn ten years ago. The hat and the clothes were not from 1910—they were from the 1930s.

Like a snake, the truth of my discovery slithered from some dark recess of my mind while I stood frozen, aghast yet fascinated by what I had released.

My house must have been vacant ten years ago—it had been vacant often during the Depression. Had Geraldine Blackstock had a key and used the Lorch house as a place in which to meet her lover? Were the books I had found and burned in some way related to their trysts? Had Charles Blackstock, already suspicious of his wife, followed her, discovered the lovers and murdered them? I found myself nodding yes in answer to each of my questions.

And then afterwards Charles had sealed the alcove with the wood paneling. He was a carpenter, I remembered. He had preserved them forever, or so he thought. But why?

I shuddered. What kind of person would leave intact the evidence against himself, evidence of murder, forcing himself to live from day to day on the precipice of discovery? Each morning he must look across to this house and see it as the tomb where his wife lies, I thought, her body not displayed like a deer head on a wall, but preserved as a secret trophy—the trophy of the avenging male.

Charles was the one who had tried to frighten me away. The killing of MacArthur, the dog let loose in the yard, the unlocked bedroom door, the attempt to buy the house—all had been his doing. A tremor began in my legs and climbed to run along my spine. Where was Charles Blackstock now, this moment?

The light. The light in the back bedroom, the room where I had found the wall that did not match. I ran down the hall to the rear corridor. The light in the bedroom was still on. I switched it off. Too late? Through the windows, which were without curtains, I saw no lights on in the Blackstock house, no car in the driveway.

I sighed with relief. Charles must have gone to Middletown with Jeremy.

I walked back along the hall. Should I tell Jeremy? Tell him his own father was a murderer? I felt a surge of sympathy, of compassion for Jeremy. Wouldn't it be kinder, I thought, to call the police first, then Jeremy—to put any decision out of his hands? Yes, I'd call the police. Jeremy, I remembered, had warned me, not once, but repeatedly, to leave. Had he known the secret of the house? No—I pushed the idea away. She had been his mother.

As I took the first step down the curved stairway I heard a sound from below. I stopped, unable to move, listening. Footsteps, heavy, measured, climbed closer; someone was coming up the cellar stairs. A knob rattled and the door creaked open below me, the door from the cellar into the hall. I shrank back against the wall, as far from the rail as I could get. The steps crossed the lower hall.

"Hello, anybody home?" A loud, friendly inquiry. I pressed my body to the wall. I had recognized the voice—Charles Blackstock. "Hello, Miss Medford, are you here?"

Think, Anne, I told myself, be logical. Your best chance is to make him believe nothing has happened. Charles may not have noticed the light from the back bedroom or, if he saw the light, might not have concluded his secret had been discovered. Even assuming he had been alerted by the light, if I act calm and unconcerned he might think I haven't yet found the room and he still has time to get me to leave the house. I trembled. Could I face him after what I had seen and still control my emotions?

Charles walked to the bottom of the stairway. As he looked up I took a deep breath and walked down to meet him.

"Why, Mr. Blackstock," I said, acting surprised. I meant my tone to imply "What are you doing here?"

He smiled, one hand on the carved newel post, a flashlight in the other. He wore a grey sportcoat over a grey-and-white-checked shirt with the two top buttons undone, the shirt forming a V in which I could see the curling grey hair on his chest. I stared at his hand on the post, noticed the veins ridging the back, saw the thick fingers and thick nails. A solid, powerful hand; and the man himself was solid, powerful.

When I stopped several steps above him he looked up into my eyes. I met his gaze. Just when I thought my lips would begin to quiver so I must turn away, he glanced over his shoulder to the open cellar door.

"I've got the fire banked for the night," he said.

"Thank you." My voice was tremulous in my ears, but he gave no sign he noticed.

"On my way over," he went on, "I saw some loose shingles on your roof from the storm last weekend. I'm going up to the attic to take a look." Too dark, I thought. The night was too dark for him to notice the condition of the roof. He must be using the shingles as an excuse to reach the upper floors of the house to find out how much I had discovered. He climbed to where I stood blocking his way.

"Why don't you come back another time?" I asked. "I'm just getting ready for bed."

His brown eyes lingered on my blouse and slacks. "You've got to take care of shingles right away," he said. "Once the rain gets in the wood rots, and instead of needing a few shingles you'll be faced with a whole new roofing job."

"It's too dark for you to do any work tonight."

"Got to see what tools I might need for the job," he said. "I won't be able to do any of the repairs tonight, you're right, but you know I told your father I'd look after things here and I should get started on that roof."

"Why don't you come over first thing in the morning?" I suggested.

He shrugged and started to turn away. I relaxed. Before I could stop him he suddenly brushed by me, climbing the stairs two at a time. I reached out to hold him. Too late. I ran in pursuit, but Charles was already at the top of the stairs. Had I left my bedroom door open?

When I entered the upper hall I found him standing in the doorway to my bedroom. I looked past him into the bedroom to the black gap where I had removed the boards. Charles faced me and I backed away until I felt the knob of the attic door on the small of my back.

"Still remodeling, I see," he said. He frowned, but his voice was casual. "Sometimes I think folks make too many alterations in these old houses. Often they're best left exactly the way you find them."

I held my breath; I couldn't speak, I could only stand, mouth open, and stare at him. Charles Blackstock sighed. "You found them, didn't you?"

I nodded almost automatically, as though I had no choice. He smiled, a forced smile, a quick nervous gesture without mirth. "I thought you would," he said. "From the first day you came here I knew you'd find them. I figured you for a girl who'd meddle where she didn't belong."

He closed his eyes, wincing as if he felt a stab of pain. He pressed his fingers to his forehead just above the bridge of his nose. Get away, I told myself. I wanted to run toward the front door, but realized he would be on me before I reached the top of the stairs. The attic. The attic was my only chance. I moved my hand along the crack of the door behind my back. I felt the bottom of the metal doorknob fixture, inched my hand higher until at last I touched the protruding key.

Charles shook his head and opened his eyes. He reached inside his coat and brought out a pistol with a long black barrel and an ivory grip. He looked fondly at the gun. "I'll have to kill you," he said, sounding as though he had just announced the need for a new washer in a faucet.

Moving only my fingers I turned the key in the lock until I felt resistance as the bolt began to slide. "Why did you do it?" I asked at the same moment I turned the key.

Charles's eyes looked over the gun to my face. I held my breath, then relaxed when I was sure my words had masked the click of the lock. "In the Old West," he said, "there were only two kinds of women: those you marry and the other kind. Gerry was the other kind. She brought misery to everyone who knew her—to me, to her son, even to those others, the men, all of them." He motioned back into the bedroom with his head. "We're all better off without her."

"Her son is better off?" I turned my fingers until the key slid from the lock. The metal was hard and cold in my grasp.

"Jeremy? Is Jeremy better off? I thought he would be. Yes, he should be. I don't know. He was never my Jeremy, you know, always *her* Jeremy." He seemed to talk to himself, the words mumbled and indistinct. He placed his thumb on the hammer of the gun and pressed down until the weapon cocked.

I noticed a movement behind him in the bedroom. Tojo stalked to the door, where he paused when he saw Charles's leg blocking his path. The cat crawled between the door and Charles, his body rubbing against Charles's leg. Charles started, jumped away while bringing his hands down to defend himself. The gun went off with a flash, a roar, a blinding billow of smoke.

# Chapter 16

Opening the attic door as I turned, I stumbled to the second step and pulled the door shut behind me. The acrid smoke stung my eyes and through tears I fumbled the key into the keyhole. Then I locked the door. As I ran up the stairs I stretched over my head to pull the light cord. At the top I leaned on the railing, my heart racing. Below I heard a thud, a yowl, whimpers fading farther and farther from me.

The doorknob at the foot of the attic stairs rattled.

How long would the locked door bar Charles's pursuit? I looked above my head to the single frosted bulb. Could I use the light as a signal? What was the Morse code for SOS? The only code I knew was the dot-dot-dot-dash of V for Victory. I reached far over the stairwell until my fingers closed on the cord. On-off, on-off, on-off I clicked the light.

Would Charles shoot off the lock? I heard a rasping sound from below—no, he must be using my screwdriver to force the door. On-off, on-off, on-off, on—I stopped at the sound of wood splintering below me.

I yanked the light cord so the light clicked off and I held the cord taut, pulled until the string snapped and dropped from my hand into the stairwell. Now the only light came through the windows from the starlit night outside. I ran past the first chimney, deep into the attic, and stopped to peer through the darkness at the roof. Yes, just as I had remembered, a black rectangle, the trapdoor halfway between the peak and the eaves. I pushed a chest of drawers under the door to the roof. I frowned. Not high enough. Lifting a chair I laid it on top of the chest.

I pulled out two drawers a few inches and used them as a ladder to climb onto the chest; I righted the chair and stepped onto it. The recessed door was on a level with my head. I pushed outward, but the wooden panel did not move. Behind and below me I heard a crack and a thump as the door into the attic sprung open. Footsteps pounded on the stairs and a beam of light probed from the stairwell. With my fingers I felt the edges of the trapdoor, found a round projection of a bolt, then the knobbed handle, tugged and twisted until the bolt rasped open. I shoved upward and felt the panel lift. Placing both palms on the bottom surface I pushed again until the door slid out and down onto the roof.

As I pulled myself through the opening my blouse caught and tore. Below I heard Charles stumbling over furniture. For a moment I sat on the roof beside the opening, the pulse in my temple throbbing, the cold air sharp in my throat. Above me a chimney tilted precariously against the sky. I clambered up the metal shingles to the chimney and looked back to see the top of Charles's head emerge from the trapdoor ten feet below me.

With one hand clutching the chimney I tugged at the bricks until I found one I could shift. I grasped the loose brick with both hands, yanked, and almost lost my balance as it pulled free. I turned and braced myself against the chimney. Charles, his back to me, gripped the sides of the opening with both hands as he pulled himself to the roof.

I raised the brick over my head and hurled it at him with all my strength. The missle struck his right shoulder and he grunted, twisting in surprise and pain. I heard a clatter from the attic underneath him and his head dropped from sight. One of his hands clutched the side of the opening and I held my breath while his fingers slid inch by inch from the casing. He fell.

Crouched, my left hand touching the high side of the roof, I clambered toward one of the gables, spurred on by the sound of Charles moving furniture in the attic below me. My feet slipped and I slid, fingers clawing at the shingles until my body held to the roof and I lay breathless, my palms stinging, an ache in my side. Looking back I saw a shadow move from the direction of the trapdoor and I knew Charles was once more climbing to the roof.

I moved sideways, crablike, until I reached the gutter next to the gable. I backed down to the edge of the roof, where I turned to look over the side at the dark balcony below. How far? Ten feet, I thought, maybe more.

Rolling over onto my stomach, I pushed with hands and knees until my feet hung over the edge of the roof. I inched my way down, felt my blouse crawl up, letting the cold shingles sting my bare flesh. My knees extended from the roof, then my hips, and my body hung suspended over nothingness. I shoved myself into a space until only my shoulders and arms clung to the shingles. I looked back to see Charles Blackstock, standing beside the chimney, turning the flashlight first one way and then another as he searched for me among the peaks and valleys of the roof.

I hung by my fingers with my entire body suspended in midair. The balcony seemed so far below. I took a deep breath, let go and for an eternity fell free. My feet slammed onto the balcony floor, and I sprawled backward. As I tried to stand, one hand on the floor, I heard a scrambling on the roof above me.

"Oh!" When I put weight on my right foot pain sliced up my leg from the ankle and I moaned, stumbled, almost fell. Clutching the balcony rail, I felt it lurch outward. I released my hold and limped to the door of my bedroom. I tested the ankle and, though it was painful, I found I could walk. My stomach stung from sliding over the shingles and my blouse gaped open.

In the bedroom I saw my purse on the bureau; I reached inside and slipped the keyring into my pocket. I glanced at the black gap in the wall and, though my queasiness returned, I could not look away. I stared, immobile. A noise from outside startled me, breaking the trance, and I limped to the hall door where I listened, but heard nothing. Charles must still be on the roof. I eased into the dim hallway and tiptoed down the curving stairs to the front door. Hope surged through me. I opened the door slowly so I would make no sound.

Brutus leaped. Jerking back I slammed the door shut, heard the dog snarl and fling himself at the obstacle. He clawed at the bottom of the door. My pulse racing, I stumbled back into the hall. My ankle throbbed. I leaned on the post at the foot of the stairs, gasping for breath. Still no sound came from the house above. How could I get out without Brutus barring the way? I knew I couldn't. Where, then, could I hide?

I heard a shrill clamor of sound. I jumped. Again the ring, insistent, jarring. The telephone. I peered at the table in the dim light, made out the silhouette of the phone. The ringing seemed a signal from another world. As though mesmerized I counted the rings under my breath, four, five, six. With a gasp of realization I pushed myself away from the post and ran to pick up the receiver.

"Hello, hello," I said.

I heard a click followed by a steady hum. Too late. Slowly I returned the receiver to the hook. The clock ticked in the recess under the stairs. The PTA meeting should be over. Had Don called to see why I wasn't there?

The phone. I picked up the receiver again. No answer. Steps sounded from the attic stairs. I juggled the hook, desperate, but still the operator did not respond. I looked around me. The cellar door was open. The fuses were in the cellar. If I could get to the fuse box I could throw the house into darkness. Laying the phone receiver on the table, I limped down the stairs a step at a time, cautiously, making no noise. A faint red glow from the furnace flickered on the fuse box. I opened the cabinet door and reached for the first fuse. Then I stopped, my hand still extended.

If I removed the fuses Charles would know where I was, where I must be. I would be trapped in the cellar, for there was only one stairway. The two windows were the only other exits; both were high on the wall at the front of the house—and at the front of the house, Brutus waited.

Steps tapped on the stairs over my head. Charles was coming down to the first floor. No time to leave the cellar now—I must hide. The heat from the fire warmed my back and, turning, I faced the furnace and heard the crackle of the flames within.

I glanced around the cellar to the workbenches, the tool chest, the lumber piled on the floor, the wire-mesh cabinets that must have once stored preserves, the pipes across the ceiling, the wooden sides of the coal bin. The coal bin. As I limped to the opening small flakes of coal gritted under my feet. The shovel hung on a nail to one side. Just inside the bin the coal was piled only a foot or two deep, but it sloped up to the side and back almost to the ceiling.

I swung one foot and then the other over the board

at the bottom of the opening and felt my shoes sink into the coal. As I moved to the side to get out of sight, the coal slid down from the pile toward me; it crunched beneath my shoes and I felt the lumps press on my ankles. I huddled against the inside of the bin. Behind me on the ceiling I saw a wooden chute jutting down toward the top of the piled coal. I bent over to look up the chute. The top was dark—a lid must cover the outside. Could I crawl over the coal to the chute, I wondered, and force my way out as I had escaped from the attic to the roof? No, I had nothing to help me climb, nothing to give me a footing on the shifting mass of coal. And in the yard Brutus waited.

The cellar light snapped on. I held my breath and pressed my body closer to the splintered boards of the bin. The siding was warped and a slit of light showed between two of the boards. Lifting my head a few inches I looked through the crack and saw the whitewashed walls, the bottom of the two windows and the door to the furnace.

Slow, cautious footsteps descended the stairs. Although I twisted my head I could not see past the bulk of the furnace. The tap, tap of Charles's boots reached the cellar floor. He paused. Had I left the fuse box open? Would he notice? I heard him cross the floor to the furnace and I could see him. His face was set, pale; and although he did not carry the gun I thought I saw a bulge beneath his jacket.

He took a metal rod about a foot and a half long from somewhere below my line of vision and approached the furnace, rod in hand, holding himself stiffly as though he was in pain. Charles leaned in front of the firebox—I could see only the upper portion of his body—and appeared to insert and shake the rod. He repeated the shaking and I heard metallic clankings as he made adjustments to the furnace door. What was he doing? Had he abandoned his pursuit of me, at least for the moment? What was more important to him than finding the only witness who could link him to the double murder?

I think we both heard the noise at the same time, the sound rising above the hiss of the flames—the deep thrum of a car. He stood erect and turned off the hanging light. I concentrated on the purr of the approaching car as it drove along the driveway toward us. Had Mrs. Allison returned?

The car slowed; it had entered the circle in front of the house and the white glare of the first headlight swung across the cellar window. I waited for the second headlight, but, though the car kept turning, the second light did not appear. Don, I thought. Don's car—he still hasn't fixed the light. He was here to see why I hadn't gone to the PTA meeting—he must have been the one who'd called.

Charles Blackstock moved swiftly. He boosted himself onto one of the workbenches, pulling aside the piece of wood Jeremy had placed in front of the broken window. He whistled, a short, high-pitched call. Brakes squealed, the motor stopped and I heard the slam of the car door. Don must have parked in front of the porch steps. The dog, I whispered. Don, watch out for the dog.

The sound of panting came from just outside the broken window. Charles spoke to Brutus in low soothing tones. He must, I thought, be holding the dog in check so Don will get no hint anything is wrong. I heard steps cross the front porch. Chimes rang in the hall above.

Had I locked the front door after I slammed it against Brutus? I couldn't remember. Would Don try to enter the house? Were there any clues to tell him something was amiss? The light, I knew, still burned in my bedroom. Wouldn't he wonder why I didn't answer the phone or the door when he saw the light? No, I realized, he doesn't even know which room is mine. The chimes rang again and I heard Don stamp his feet as though they were cold, then pace back and forth on the porch and stop, perhaps to peer through a window or one of the glass panels beside the door.

Should I cry out to him, climb from the bin and run to the stairs? How far would I get before Charles was upon me? He would hear me, certainly, as I scrambled from the coal, catch me at the foot of the cellar stairs. Would Don hear? If he did, what could he do against an armed man, a man who had killed twice and showed no hesitation about killing again? The chimes rang, a steady, vibrating ring as though Don was pushing the button steadily, without pause. The echo of the chimes faded, the house creaked, the fire hissed. I listened to my quick, frantic breathing.

Don's steps crossed the porch. Did I hear the crunch of gravel as he walked along the drive? The car door opened and closed and in a moment the engine roared. I glanced at Charles Blackstock. He had not moved from the spot where he knelt on the workbench, body tense, his eyes staring away from me into the night.

The car rounded the circle of the drive and the sound of the motor grew fainter and fainter until I could no longer hear it. I felt a sinking inside of me, a sense of despair, of being hopelessly alone. The cellar seemed warmer and the crackle of the fire louder. Charles swung his feet from the bench and dropped to the floor, lifting the wooden panel back over the window. From outside I could hear Brutus' snarl, and then the dog was gone.

Charles turned and walked directly toward my hiding place.

# Chapter 17

Charles Blackstock turned on the light, then took the shovel from the outside of the bin and used the blade to lift and pull open the furnace door. He had not seen me. Through the crack between the boards I saw flames leap inside the firebox, the heat forcing Charles to back away. For a minute or two he mumbled to himself as he watched the flames; then he slammed the door shut. He laid the shovel on the floor, walked across the room and went up the stairs.

What should I do? I was afraid to climb through
the cellar window, afraid of Brutus. If I tried to reach
the phone I could easily meet Charles, for now I had
no idea where in the house he was or what he was doing.
I stayed where I was.

After what seemed an endless time Charles returned
to open the door from the hall and descend the stairs,
more slowly than before, step by step, stopping often
as though he carried a heavy burden. When he reached
the cellar floor he paused, and I heard a soft thump
followed by a sliding, scraping noise. I saw him as he
walked backwards around the furnace with his shoulders
and arms straining to pull something across the floor.
I noticed he no longer wore his jacket. I had been right—
he carried the gun in a holster under his right arm. When
Charles was some ten feet beyond my hiding place he
squatted and lifted his burden onto a workbench outside
the range of my vision.

Once more he climbed the stairs, still talking to himself,
his voice louder now. After his footsteps faded in the
upper reaches of the house I leaned my head against
the rough wood siding of the bin and shut my eyes.
I felt trapped, enclosed by the heat, by the black mass
of the coal, by Charles. My whole body ached and my
ankle throbbed. A weariness engulfed me, a stupor in
which I felt the oppressive heat from the furnace and
in which I was able to observe Charles's every action—but
in which I was prevented from thinking or acting.

Charles came back and repeated the slow descent
of the stairs, the dragging of something across the floor,
the lifting of the burden onto the same bench. He slumped
against the workbench, breathing hard until he regathered
his strength. Finally he walked away. I thought he would
climb the stairs again, but instead he crossed the room
to the tool chest. When he came back he carried something in his hand, but I couldn't see what it was.

Perspiration trickled down my forehead, smarted in
my eyes. My clothes clung damply to my body. Carefully,
slowly taking out a handkerchief, I wiped my face. The
cloth came away soiled with coal dust.

From the workbench a steady rasp began, the sound of a saw hacking back and forth, back and forth. Charles must be having difficulty with his task, for he swore and laid the saw aside, and he appeared to rearrange his work. Once he stopped completely and strode to the far side of the cellar, clenched his right hand and struck the wall, with his fist, hard—once, twice, three times. Then he leaned on the wall, motionless, his forehead resting on the back of his hand. At last he stood erect, rubbed his palms on his trousers and walked to the bench where he resumed cutting, first with long, slow strokes, then with a fast ripping sound.

Charles again came toward my hiding place; he bent and grasped the wooden handle of the shovel. Even from where I huddled in the bin I felt the wave of heat when he opened the furnace door. My skin prickled and I shrank away, covering my face with my hands.

He carried an armload of what appeared to be sawed-up kindling from his workbench to the furnace. Standing several feet from the fire, which now roared, he tossed the things, one by one, underhand, into the flames. An occasional log, if truly they were logs, missed the rectangular opening, struck the side of the furnace and clumped to the floor. When the last object had sizzled on the fire, Charles used the shovel to scoop the others from the floor and flip them into the flames.

Did I know what Charles fed into the furnace? Yes, of course. On the other hand, no, not really. My mind was satiated, overflowing with horror. I could accept no more, would accept no more, so I rejected the meaning of what I saw.

The blazing coals crackled. The flames became yellow as they licked over the new fuel and finally sucked the unburnt fragments down amongst the coals. Charles shut the furnace door and stood, sweat glistening on his face, with his back to me. Only the thin boards of the coal bin separated us. Through the crack I saw the soiled grey tweed of his trousers.

"You're going to the movies with Helen?" he asked. I started, for I feared he was talking to me, but when

I sorted out the sense of his words I knew he was not. He spoke with the slow and patient tone of a parent speaking to a young child.

"Yes, yes," he said, "I don't mind, go ahead." He laughed. "Gerry, you're so stupid, so damned stupid. But this, Gerry, this?" He pushed himself away from the side of the bin and paced from one wall of the cellar to the other with his hands clenching and unclenching at his sides.

"The gun's no good," he muttered. "Not the way at all. I've got to think, use my head. The balcony. The railing's almost shot. Should have fixed that railing a long time back. Just as well now I didn't. She went out on the balcony because the dog was in the yard, leaned on the rail, fell and broke her neck." He paced, his words again indistinct, then he stopped and faced the furnace.

"Gerry!" he called. His voice was a hoarse shout. He whispered, "Gerry, Gerry," and I thought he sobbed. "I didn't want it to end here, Gerry, like this. Why didn't you leave me a way out? Why did you always do the wrong thing at the wrong time?" He wiped his face with a large red bandanna. "Gerry," he said in a conversational tone, "sometimes I wonder if this isn't what you wanted all along."

Charles walked to the bench and for a few minutes I could hear only an occasional meaningless word. He returned to the fire with what seemed to be a bundle in his arms. "A union man," he said with disdain. "Gerry, you never had any class. An out-of-town troublemaker's all he was. And Giles Henry. You told me about Giles Henry, remember? How could you expect me to forgive you, ever, after Giles Henry?"

Charles laid his bundle on the floor and opened the furnace again. He stooped below the range of my sight and then began tossing pieces of cloth into the flames.

The last item seemed to be a blanket; it did not go through the opening, so Charles took the shovel to push it inside. Too late. Flames blazed up over the blanket, caught on the splintered beams over his head. Charles beat at the fire with the shovel. Thick, acrid smoke spread across the ceiling. My throat tickled and I swallowed so I would not cough. At last Charles snagged the burning blanket with the shovel and stuffed it into the furnace. He ran to the far side of the room and came back with a broom; with this he beat at the small tongues of flame on the beams until they smoked and died.

He used the broom to sweep up around the furnace and the bench; he pushed the litter into the shovel and threw it on the fire. Then Charles came to the bin and thrust the shovel in less than a foot from where I crouched, the coal grating on the metal. He hurled a shovelful of coal into the pulsing fire—then another and another until the virgin coal covered the flames so they seethed and hissed once more. He slammed the furnace door.

Returning the shovel to the nail on the outside of the bin, he wiped his hands on his trousers. He stood in the center of the open space between bin and furnace and looked around the room. Satisfied, he walked away, around the furnace, and climbed the stairs. For a moment I heard him in the first floor hall; then the house was quiet.

I waited. I did not move. When no sound came from above I relaxed, laying my head against the board. Spots spun in wild ellipses before my eyes. After a time I seemed to drift; I knew the pleasant sensation of drowsing in a boat on a quiet lake in midsummer. I floated. All I wanted to do was float and float and float forever. Was that noise the splashing of water? No, a different sound, more like a scratching. Leave me alone, I whispered, let me lie here forever and ever.

Again the scratching. Reluctantly, I opened my eyes. Tojo's green irises stared at me, the eyes seeming disembodied so closely did his black fur blend with the coal. He approached cautiously and rubbed along my leg. I reached to him, felt his warm softness under my hand, the quivering life of his body.

I gripped the edge of the bin and pulled myself up until I sat leaning against the vertical timber framing the opening of the bin. The cat leaped down to the floor, stopped and looked back at me. I stood, unsteady, ankle hurting, but I forced myself to limp past the fire and follow Tojo to the stairs.

When we reached the top step I knelt and scooped the cat into my arms. Holding him to my side I eased open the door with my other hand. The first floor was dark and quiet, the only sound the ticking of the clock.

"The phone, Tojo," I whispered. I waited until my eyes were accustomed to the dark before I crossed to the hall table with the cat cradled on my chest. I picked up the receiver, which had been put back on its hook. I heard no hum, no sound at all—the phone was dead. With a sigh I replaced the receiver. Going to the front door I peered through the glass panel and saw the porch, my car a dark bulk to the left, the drive a grey circle in front of me, and beyond the drive shadows from the shrubs stretching toward the house.

For a moment I stroked the cat and felt comforted by the sound and vibration of his purring. I smiled. I felt stronger and my mind seemed to have cleared. I noticed a movement on the driveway—Brutus. The dog stopped with his nose in the air and looked toward the house as though he sensed my presence behind the door. "Once more," I whispered to the cat. "You've got to help me once more."

I turned the knob and pushed the door open. The night air struck me like a cold slap. Kneeling in the narrow opening I held Tojo on the floor with both hands. His body tensed under my fingers as he saw, or sensed, the nearness of the dog. He squirmed as he tried to push back into the house, but I tightened my hold. Brutus took a few tentative steps in our direction, stopped, his body poised and ready to spring forward.

I pushed Tojo onto the porch to my right. He hesitated, reluctant to leave the safety of the house, but then scuttled along the porch next to the wall. The Doberman charged. Tojo jumped to the rail some twenty feet from me and clawed his way up the post; the dog raced across the porch in pursuit. Brutus placed both front paws on the rail and snarled up at the huddled cat.

I slipped through the door with my eyes on Brutus, tiptoed down the steps, thankful for the rubber soles of my saddle shoes, and limped, glancing behind me at the dog, over the wet earth between driveway and porch. Putting my hand in my pocket, I groped for the right key. I should have had the key ready, I realized, but I had forgotten.

The dog dropped from the rail and trotted to the porch steps. Had he heard me? I kept walking. I had the key now, its square end clasped between my fingers. The car was only a few feet away. The dog hurtled to the ground, skidded on the gravel of the drive, recovered and lunged at me. Put the key in the lock, I told myself, put the key in the lock. There. Turn backwards. Hurry. Open the door. Sliding into the driver's seat I pulled the door shut as the dog jumped against the car, snarling. I looked through the window at his dark face inches from mine. A thread of saliva was hanging from his jaw, his white teeth were glinting in the dim light.

I turned the key in the ignition. The motor ground, once, twice, but did not start. I glanced up at the house; I thought I saw a light high above. Touching the gas pedal with my foot I turned the key again. The engine roared. Shift into reverse, I told myself. I backed toward the porch steps. Go into forward. The gear engaged. Pressing too hard on the accelerator I made the Dodge lurch ahead, but the car did not stall. As I rounded the circle I saw the dog lope straight across the lawn to wait for me where the drive curved toward the street.

I gripped the steering wheel with both hands. I was free to drive from the yard and follow Spruce Street to the five corners, where I would find Harry Riley, the village policeman. I was sure he would be there, sitting in his car beside Santoro's, for Thursday nights, like most other nights, were quiet in Canterbury. He'd probably call in the state troopers from their barracks in Monroe. Charles Blackstock would be caught and imprisoned.

Brutus stood beside the turn in the drive waiting to run yapping after the car. A rage toward the dog surged through me and for the first time in my life I felt hate. I pressed the gas pedal and swerved the car. The dog yelped as he lunged away in surprise, but he was too late. The car shot ahead and the front right bumper slammed into Brutus high on his chest. I heard a thud and for a moment I saw the dog hang suspended on the front of the car—then he fell to the ground.

I stamped on the brake and the car slid in the mud, still moving ahead, and I felt the back wheel bump over something. The car rocked from side to side and I tried to turn it back onto the drive. The branches of a shrub scraped my door and the car skidded to a stop. With my foot on the clutch I shifted back into first, pressed on the gas, listened in dismay to the whine of the back wheels spinning helplessly in the mud. Glancing back to the house I saw lights not only in the attic, but also shining onto the lawn from the first floor. I remembered the gun with the black barrel and the ivory grip.

I sat rigid, the car idling while I tried desperately to recall what to do when caught in the mud. Traction, I remembered. Pile brush beneath the wheels for traction. I looked out into the night, afraid to leave the sanctuary of the locked car. I backed slowly, ever so slowly, into the bush behind me. When I felt the resistance of the branches under the rear wheels, I shifted into first, the wheels grabbed on the limbs and the car spurted ahead. Again the right rear wheel bumped and then both back wheels spun in the mud while the front tires sent gravel clattering under the fenders. But then all at once the car leaped ahead onto the driveway.

I glanced over my shoulder to where a dark mass lay unmoving alongside the driveway. I felt sick and nauseated, yet I also knew an elation, an overriding sense of triumph. Brutus was dead. I should, I told myself, feel ashamed because of my joy. I did not—I was glad he was dead.

I braked at the end of the drive and turned left into Spruce Street. Beyond the streetlight a large black car emerged from between the pillars of the Blackstock drive, turned toward me and slowed, then stopped about a hundred feet in front of me. A tall man jumped from the car and ran to the middle of my lane waving his arms.

As my foot reached for the brake I recognized Jeremy.

# Chapter 18

I slowed the car and stopped. Jeremy walked quickly around to my door. As I rolled the window down a few inches I heard the idling motor of his car. When I pushed hair from my face I saw my hands and clothes were black from the coal. I tried without success to pull my torn blouse together.

"Anne, are you all right?" Jeremy asked, anxiety in his tone.

"Yes," I told him. I couldn't keep the quaver from my voice. Suddenly I trembled—my legs, my arms, my entire body; it was a trembling I was unable to control. I pulled up the lock button and Jeremy swung the car door open. He half lifted, half slid me from the seat, and with a sob I buried my face in his chest and felt his protecting hands firm on my back.

"I . . . I was so afraid," I stammered as I held myself to him. He murmured my name over and over into my hair.

At last the trembling stopped. I felt enveloped in the warmth of him. Jeremy took a handkerchief from his pocket and wiped the tears from my face; then he shrugged out of his jacket and draped it over my shoulders. He held me by my upper arms.

"Can you tell me what happened?" he asked. I started to speak, sobbed, leaned against him once more. "The operator called," he said. "Your phone's off the hook

and she asked if I'd stop by to make sure everything
was all right."

"Your father," I said. I swallowed, took a deep breath
and moved back a step. How could I tell him? Charles
was his father, Gerry his mother. How could I tell him
his father had . . . ? His fingers tightened on my arms.
"He tried to kill me," I said.

"Kill you?" Jeremy sounded incredulous.

"The room. Behind the paneling. He killed them,
walled them in, he . . . " Was I making sense? Jeremy
shook me, hard, so my head jerked back. I squeezed
my eyes shut until they hurt. Suddenly I was calmer.
"Your father must have been watching. All these weeks
watching the house, the lights, watching me." I stopped
again. "He saw the light," I said. "He suspected what
I was doing. When he saw I'd been in the room he was
going to kill me. He burned them in the furnace. I got
away."

Jeremy's face was pale in the glow from the streetlight.
"Who did he kill?" he asked.

"Your mother and her . . . your mother and a man.
I don't know who he was."

I saw the muscle at the corner of his mouth twitch.
He shook his head; he appeared grim but not surprised.
"I was afraid of something like that," he said.

"You knew?"

"No, never. But I wondered what had happened to
my mother. Wouldn't you? Wouldn't anyone? I knew
she'd never leave without a word to me, no matter what
Charles said."

"I think he's out of his mind. He mumbled and talked
to himself, even talked to her. To . . . to your mother."
I stopped, heard again the rasp of the saw and Charles's
footsteps pacing back and forth; felt again the searing
heat of the fire.

"Where is he?" Jeremy looked over my head and
I turned in his arms, but could see only the row of
evergreens along the street, the crouched shrubs and
the dark roof of the house.

"He?" I asked.

"Charles. Where is Charles?"

"Now? I don't know. He was searching through the house for me."

"He must have heard your car."

"I'm sure he did. I thought I saw lights come on downstairs when I drove away."

"He probably went back to our house." Jeremy dropped one hand to his side while he led me to my car with the other. "Go for the police," he said. "I don't see any way out. I'll try to find him."

"He's got a gun."

"So do I." Jeremy placed his hand on the butt of a pistol under his belt. He turned to walk to his car, but stopped after he'd gone a few feet.

"Brutus," he said. "Have you seen Brutus?"

My fingers clenched on the edge of the car door. "Yes." I hesitated, did not meet his eyes. "Brutus is dead. My car hit him."

"Your car? You ran over Brutus with the car?"

"He chased the cat, he attacked me, he would have killed me." How could I make him understand?

Jeremy crossed his arms and I saw his fingers knead the sleeves of his shirt. "Brutus would never kill anybody. He might grab hold of a trespasser, nothing more."

"The dog's a killer," I said. I felt tears burn my eyes.

"You're the one who's the killer."

My face flushed with anger. "You seem more upset by what happened to that damned dog than you do about your own mother!" The words were out before I could stop them.

Jeremy's mouth tightened. He stepped to me and slapped me hard across the face so my head snapped to one side, my cheek stinging. I put my face in my hands and sobbed. I tried to stop, dug fingernails into my forehead, but the tears ran down my cheeks.

Jeremy stood in front of me and I could hear his rapid breathing. He moved and I flinched away but he didn't touch me. He sighed. No, it wasn't a sigh; it was more a shudder than a sigh.

"I'm sorry," he said.

"You're always sorry afterwards," I told him.

"I don't . . ." he began.

"I'm . . . " I said at the same time. We both stopped. I lowered my hands to see his head jerk up and turn. On the far side of the streetlight Charles walked from my driveway to the road, his white hair disarranged, his face streaked. He did not wear a jacket. The pistol still protruded from the holster under his arm.

"Get behind the car," Jeremy said in an urgent whisper. He walked past the back of my car to face Charles while I knelt next to the front bumper and peered over the fender at the two men. This, I realized, was only the second time I had ever seen them together. They looked nothing alike—Charles, though almost as tall as his son, was heavyset, massive, solid, while Jeremy was thin and lithe.

The two men walked toward one another until they were about forty feet apart. They stopped in the center of the street with the telephone pole and streetlight halfway between them.

"Come home with me," Jeremy said, each word distinct.

Charles shook his head. "She was no good!" he shouted. "I did what I had to do."

"It's over and done with. Come home."

"It will never be done with as long as I'm alive," Charles said, "or as long as you are. You don't understand, boy."

"I understand better than you think." Jeremy's voice was low and he seemed tired. "I know about Giles Henry."

Charles didn't answer at once. He grimaced, seemed confused. He pushed his hair back from his forehead with one hand. "Giles Henry?" he repeated.

"I know who Giles Henry was and about him and my mother. I know what Giles Henry is to me."

"How could you know?"

"I heard you, you and mother. The next day I saw the bruises on her face and neck. She said she fell on the stairs. I wanted to kill you."

"She was no good. She was a curse visited on everyone who knew her."

"Why didn't you leave her, then? I always wondered why you stayed in spite of everything. And why she stayed with you. What kept you together?"

"I wish to God I knew." Charles's voice was so low I had to strain to hear. "Sometimes I thought I was crazy, or that she was. It was almost as though we both needed to have someone to hate. Does that make sense, boy? Or maybe I loved her, in a way. Could you believe I loved her?"

"You never loved anybody but yourself."

"You don't know, Jeremy. There's no way on this green earth for you to know what was between your mother and me."

"You had no right to kill her."

"Right? Nobody had a better right. After I found out about Giles? After our bargain? I kept my part, I've kept my part all these years. You know I have."

"Your part? What bargain?"

"Don't you know? You seem to know so much! My bargain to raise you as my son. No one knows you're not. No one need ever know. Stand aside. I know the girl's behind the car."

"Anne Medford isn't involved. This is between you and me."

"You're wrong. She's like Gerry. I knew from the first day she'd bring trouble. She interfered where she had no right."

"Anne meant no harm."

Charles reached across his chest and pulled the pistol from its holster. "Stand aside," he told Jeremy again. He began to walk, slow and stiff, toward us. Step by step Jeremy backed away until he stood against the rear bumper of the car. His hand moved up to the pistol in his belt.

Charles's gun roared. A star of shattered glass radiated from a small black hole in the rear window of the Dodge. I dropped to the street, felt the gravel bite into my knees and palms. Another shot. The bullet ricocheted off the macadam.

I looked up. Jeremy knelt on one knee in the street, gun in his right hand, left elbow braced on his knee with his left hand steadying his shooting arm. Another shot. Jeremy's arm jerked back from the recoil. I heard a grunt, then a scrabbling on the gravel. I couldn't see. Jeremy stood with his back to me and shouted, but I couldn't make out the words. Gunsmoke drifted toward me. Far down on the other side of the street a house light snapped on, then another and another.

I crawled on hands and knees from the shelter of the car and stood up, my legs unsteady. Jeremy ran toward a motionless form on the street beneath the light. Charles. I thought of the huddled mass of Brutus. Now Charles. I ran after Jeremy and reached him as he knelt beside the older man.

"He's breathing," Jeremy said. Charles, face down, mumbled. Jeremy bent to him. I trembled and stepped back, my arms clamped tight across my chest. A breeze off the river sighed through the evergreens.

"What?" Jeremy's ear almost touched the other man's lips. I shivered, felt dizzy, thought I would fall. Jeremy glanced up at me. "Go and . . . " he said. I closed my eyes and covered my face with my hands.

Jeremy put his hands under Charles's arms and dragged him to the brown grass along the road. He grasped my wrist. "Come on," he said. He pulled me to my car, shoved me in, slid in after me to sit behind the wheel. I leaned my head on the cold glass of the window on the passenger side.

The key was still in the ignition. The wheels scattered gravel as Jeremy started the car, accelerated, swung between the pillars into his driveway. Behind us on the street I saw the unmoving beams of the headlights of his car. We skidded to a stop in front of the porch. He flung the car door open. "No," I whispered. "Don't leave me."

He ran around the front of the car to my side and opened the door. With his fingers urgent on my arm

we crossed the porch and went through the hall to the
den where Jeremy released me. He turned on the light
with one hand while he picked up the phone with the
other. I stumbled to an armchair and sank into the dark
leather. Antlers seemed to clutch at me from the deer
head over the fireplace. I looked away. Behind the door
to the hall I saw the framed photograph of a young man
and a young woman. Charles and his wife. I shut my
eyes.

"Doctor? Jeremy Blackstock. There's been a shooting
accident," he said into the phone. "On Spruce Street
in the village. You'll call the ambulance? Good. A car's
on the road, they can't miss it."

I opened my eyes to see him jiggle the receiver with
his forefinger. "I want the police," he said. While he
waited he drummed his fingers on the table. "Hello,
Harry? This is Jeremy Blackstock. You'd better come
over; my father's been shot." He listened to the voice
on the other end. "Yes, I called the doctor, they're on
the way." Another pause. "Let me tell you when you
get here, O.K.?" He returned the receiver to the hook.

"Do you know what he said?" Jeremy asked. I knew
he meant Charles. I shook my head. "He was saying
my name over and over."

Jerry? I thought. Or Gerry?

"I'll go with him to the hospital." Jeremy got to his
feet. "You can stay here."

I looked at the gun cabinets on the wall. Two were
empty. Did I see a stain on the blade of the long knife?
"No, not here," I said. He was already in the hall. I
pulled his jacket about me as I hurried after him.

"The keys are in your car," he told me over his shoulder. I followed him. The branches of the pines groaned
in the wind. Jeremy, looking straight ahead, let the gate
swing shut so I had to run to catch and push it open.

"Are you all right?" I asked.

"Yes. Both of his shots went wild."

"He was hurt getting onto the roof of the house."

"That's not why he missed. Charles is a crack shot.
He could have killed me if he wanted to." We passed

his car. Farther along the street a man in a bathrobe, flashlight in his hand, watched us. In the distance a siren wailed.

Jeremy rubbed his palms on the sides of his trousers. It was the same gesture, I realized with a start, Charles had made in the cellar.

"Who was Giles Henry?" I asked. The siren seemed only a few blocks away.

"He was my father," Jeremy said without looking back. He answered as if by rote. "It's not so much who he was as what he was."

A flashing red light approached from out of the darkness. The ambulance slowed when its headlights, like the twin antennae of a carrion hunter, found Charles's body.

"What he was? I don't understand. What was Giles Henry?"

Jeremy faced me. "He was a Negro," he said.

On the road under the streetlight two men in white squatted beside Charles. The light on top of the ambulance throbbed like a pulse. From the village another siren screamed in the night.

For a moment Jeremy's words made no impression on me. Then I realized what he had said. My hand covered my mouth. "Oh my God," I said. Jeremy turned from me as though I had slapped his face.

I took a few steps away, stopped, then walked to the side of the road where the Blackstock fence ended and my yard began. "Anne, come back," Jeremy said. Get away, get away, a voice repeated in my mind. I started to run. I ran past the shrubs, past Brutus' body lying next to the ruts in the mud of the driveway. I looked back to the street to see shadowed figures move in front of the lights. I did not see Jeremy.

I stopped in front of the house. Lights shone from windows on the first floor and in the attic. The second floor was dark. As I climbed to the porch I tripped on the top step. Through the open front door I saw the dark of the hall, heard the clock tick. I pictured the gap in my bedroom wall and the musty room with

its obscene streamers of dust, saw again the red flicker
of fire reflected from Charles's face. I could not go in. I
turned away from the house. You've won, I thought.

From the street came the squeal of brakes and the
urgent murmur of men's voices. Jeremy. I couldn't go
back to Jeremy. I had nowhere left. I crossed the porch,
dizzy, reached for the post at the top of the steps, stumbled, clutched at the post and fell, pain searing at my side.
I looked up from the bottom of the steps to see a white
cat sitting statuelike on the porch above me. Fire exploded
in my mind and I felt I was being sucked into a void.
I welcomed the darkness.

# Chapter 19

Toward the end of the next week a wind from the south
brought the false promise of a return of summer. The
sky was blue, the deep blue of October, birds chattered
from the maples and through my open window I could
hear the radio from the apartment next door. Girls in
summer dresses chanted to the rhythm of a jump rope
on the sidewalk across Hudson Street; in the yard of
an old brick house two boys flipped knives into the
soft earth.

My rooms seemed small after the house, though Mrs.
Burke, the principal's wife, said they were spacious compared to some of the others in the Strause Apartments.
I had a sitting room, bedroom, kitchen and bath. I was
lucky to have the apartment. Mrs. Burke knew the former
tenant, who had moved upstate to live with her parents
after her husband was drafted. "For you, Mrs. Burke,
I'll save the apartment," Mrs. Strause had promised.
I had rented it sight unseen.

I came directly to my new home from the hospital.
Mrs. Burke, Jean and Charley, the two teachers I
sometimes lunched with, and Don moved my belongings
from the Lorch house. My possessions had always seemed

inadequate in that great house; here they filled the rooms to overflowing.

During those first few mornings I woke to frost and children on their way to school breaking the thin film of ice on the puddles along the street. After breakfast I listened to the radio or sat in my rocker next to the radiator and looked out the window at the patterns formed by the branches of the maple trees.

On one of those cold October days they buried Charles Blackstock. Only a few people attended the funeral, Jean said—Jeremy, some friends of his youth, neighbors from Spruce Street and the women who, in small towns, attend all funerals. Jean had not gone—she'd heard about the funeral from her landlady, who knew the driver of the Bevans Brothers hearse.

Then, the night after he was buried, the warm wind from the south came in. The weather was like spring and I felt discontented, I wanted to be outside—but when I took a deep breath at the open window I winced from the pull of the tape on my broken ribs.

Slowly I returned to my rocker. I knew I should write Karl. I hadn't written him in over two weeks. Tomorrow, I told myself, I'll write tomorrow. I picked up last night's paper and began to work the crossword puzzle. Eleven down, a five letter word for a sea north of Turkey. I lettered BLACK in the squares, but then laid the paper on the table. A small clock ticked on a mantel above a false fireplace. Five after four. The newspaper usually came at quarter after. I had come to look forward to the ritual of reading the evening paper.

I rocked and stared out at the shadows of late afternoon. Night comes early in October. Beyond the trees, beyond the small houses, woodsheds and garages, the dark mountain curved down to the notch made by the road and then to the river. I couldn't see the river from the apartment.

The paperboy was late, so I didn't start reading until four-thirty, which made it suppertime when I finished. I heated vegetable soup and opened a box of soda crackers. After supper I changed into a dress and sat waiting for the doorbell. It rang at seven.

"Hi," Don said. "Here, these are for you."

"They're beautiful," I told him. I took the chrysanthemums and found an empty vase in the closet. Don had visited me every evening since I'd come home from the hospital, and each time he brought flowers. I looked forward to his visits.

Jeremy had not come to see me while I was in the hospital nor had he visited me since I'd come to live in the apartment.

"Let me," Don said. He took the vase from my hands, filled it at the kitchen sink, then placed the bouquet on the mantel. For a moment we had nothing to say. Don's fingers played with the cloth of the slipcover on the arm of his chair while I rocked to and fro.

"Indian summer." Don broke the silence. "Almost every year in October we have an Indian summer. Usually it only lasts a few days."

"And after Indian summer's over?"

"The winter comes. The ponds freeze first, then the river. We might be ice skating by Thanksgiving, but even if we're not we'll have snow in November. And then the cold sets in. January and February are the worst, the months of deep cold. Why don't we go for a walk on Saturday while the weather's still warm? Will you be able to get out by then?"

"Saturday?" A memory hovered in my mind, but I could not place it. For some reason I couldn't remember everything that had happened during the last few weeks, nor did I want to. "Yes," I said, "I'd like that. There's so much of Canterbury I haven't seen, what with being busy at school and remodeling the house. And Dr. Dempsey told me I can go out now any time I want to."

"Wonderful. Don't worry about your classes. Mr. Burke said to take your time getting well. He's still teaching geometry and trig and Mrs. Hawes, she used to teach math, is coming in part time to handle the others.

Mr. Burke told me he's really impressed with how far along the students are."

'I smiled. "And the math club?"

"Going great guns. Nine members now and more joining every day. Mr. Burke's arranged a contest with Monroe for next month and there's been a suggestion that we have a county-wide math field day in the spring."

"You always bring me good news," I said.

His whole face smiled and a lock of brown hair fell over his forehead. Sometimes, as now, he seemed almost boyish. "Anne," he said, pushing the hair back with his hand, "I never want to bring you anything but good news, ever. It's the least I can do in exchange for what you've given me. You're good for me, you know. You make me feel comfortable, at ease.

"I haven't mentioned it to anybody," he said, "but I've felt kind of like a sore thumb here in Canterbury the last year or two, being the only young man on the faculty. I've wondered what people think, and what the kids think, too. Like asking why I'm not in the army or at least doing war work. I almost took another job this year. They pay awfully well in those aircraft plants on Long Island."

"I'm glad you didn't," I told him.

"I get so frustrated with teaching," Don said. "They won't listen to us, those of us who want to make changes. Burke and the rest of them want to keep schools the way they were thirty years ago."

"You're right," I said, "we need change."

"I want to try new ways, let the students have more to say about what they'll study and when and how. Like with your math field days, that was a great idea. Where did it come from? The members of the club themselves. And you'll have better luck now than if you'd imposed it on them. We can get the students involved like that in English, too, in social studies, in almost all the courses. Studies prove graduates from less regimented high schools do better in college than those from traditional schools. But no one pays any attention."

I felt a stir in me, an interest, the first I had known for days. Don, I knew, was much more complex than I had thought at first. He groped and stumbled yet he tried new ways, made things happen, didn't just talk about them. And, however circuitously, he accomplished most of what he set out to do.

When he left around nine I saw him to the door, where he leaned down and kissed me gently on the lips. I walked to the window and watched him wave as he walked to his car. I smiled when I saw he'd had the headlight fixed.

I went back to work on Monday. Eyes turned toward me in the halls, for I had gained a notoriety of a sort, but after a time I became accustomed to the stares and they stopped bothering me. The teaching went well, almost as though I had never been gone. By the end of the day, though, I was tired. Don stopped at my homeroom after the final bell, but I told him I had to drive over to see Mrs. Allison.

"I'll take a rain check," he said.

I drove with the windows down, wishing winter would never come. I parked in the circle of the driveway in front of the Lorch house—I no longer thought of it as mine. Had the house ever really been mine? I sat in the car for a moment staring at the gables, the peaks and valleys of the roof, the chimneys. I had expected to feel repelled by the house, but I did not. I felt nothing, as though all my emotion had been expended and now I had none left.

Mrs. Allison opened the door before I rang the bell. "I was expecting you," she said. "Come in, I'll fix us a nice pot of coffee."

"No, thank you," I said. I looked past her into the hall at the grandfather clock in the recess under the stairs, at the door to the cellar. "I've only got a few minutes," I said. "I wanted you to know I'm going to put the house up for sale."

"I understand."

"Maybe the next owner will want to go on renting the downstairs to you."

"I hope so," Mrs. Allison said. "Some folks might be upset by what happened and in a way I am, but I think whatever evil was in the house is gone now."

"When you write the major, will you tell him I said hello?"

"Yes, of course I will. And from now on I'll mail you the check for the rent. You're staying at the Strause Apartments, aren't you?"

"Yes, I am." I heard a noise behind me, turned and jumped back with my hand to my mouth. A white cat stared up at me from the foot of the steps.

"He does give a body a turn, doesn't he?' Mrs. Allison said. "Looks so much like MacArthur. Poor MacArthur —Jeremy told me what happened to him. I found this cat on the porch the day I came back from the city. He doesn't seem to belong to anybody so I guess I've inherited him."

I said good-bye to Mrs. Allison, walked to my car and drove onto Spruce Street. The paperboy walked from house to house throwing papers on porches. When he came to the Blackstock house he was about to thrust a rolled paper in the fence when he paused and pushed open the gate. He disappeared in the pines. I slowed, undecided, then stopped and waited until the boy came out before I stepped from the car.

The BEWARE-OF-THE-DOG sign was still on the fence. I opened the gate. The lawn needed raking and pine needles covered the gravel walk. The folded paper lay on the porch. From behind the house came an irregular thump, thump, so I walked past the parked Cadillac to the top of the slope overlooking the river.

Jeremy, in grey shirt and pants, leaped and shot a basketball one-handed at a basket mounted on a weathered backboard. The ball swished through a new white net. The basket was high on a post at one end of a cleared space bordered by pines. I watched while he dribbled over the hard-packed earth. He slowed his dribble as he sensed my presence; then he looked up and stopped with the ball in his hands. Sweat glistened on his forehead and the front of his shirt was damp.

Jeremy, face set and without expression, walked to stand in front of me. "I thought I'd better start getting in shape," he said.

"I heard you were going back to college."

"Yes, I've applied at Syracuse for the January semester. I'll be on the GI bill. Probably try out for basketball next fall."

"I'm selling my house," I said.

"So Mrs. Allison told me. That house is blighted. The sooner it's destroyed, the better."

"I'm sorry about Charles," I told him. Jeremy frowned, turned and sent the ball arching toward the basket. The ball hit the front of the rim and bounced to the ground, where it rolled to lie under one of the pines.

"Not your fault at all," he said. We walked to the crest of the slope above the river, where I sat on a wooden bench while Jeremy stood in front of me with one foot on the front slat. He looked older somehow, pale; the grey in his hair seemed more pronounced.

"Jeremy . . . " I began. I wanted to tell him how I felt, my concern for him and the suffering he had known. The words wouldn't come.

"It's almost as if the Blackstocks were cursed," he said, talking as much to himself as to me. "Every time I see things going good, there's a new disaster. My mother first, her disappearing; then the army, when I thought I'd become an officer; now this."

"What did happen in the army?" I asked. "If you want to tell me."

"There's no secret. After two years, eighteen months of them overseas, I started to have attacks where I'd lose consciousness without warning, black out. The doctors have a name for what was wrong, what still is wrong, but I don't think even they know for sure just what it is. The army gave me a medical discharge and now I report to the hospital every month for tests."

"I wondered," I said. "You know, I'll miss you when you go to college."

"I've got to get away." He turned to look down at the blue water of the Hudson. On the far shore a train sped north along the New York Central tracks. "A beautiful country," he said, then shrugged. "I'll probably sell, too. I don't think I'll come back to Canterbury to live, not ever."

"I know how you feel." I thought of my heartbreak when my father had died.

I felt an emptiness and a deep desperation, as though something terrible was happening and I was helpless to prevent it. "Jeremy," I said, "I love you."

He still faced the river. I saw his body tense and he turned and I looked into his brown eyes, feeling the sting of tears in mine. The muscle in the corner of his mouth twitched.

"Don't, Anne," he said. "I can't. I'm as blighted as your house. I'm crippled. Not because of my father, my real father—the wound goes deeper, it's within me, beyond reach. I can't love you, I can't love anyone. I wish I could—I wanted to. I've tried, God knows I've tried, but I can't. All I'd bring you would be pain."

"Shouldn't I decide?"

"No," he said. "It's been decided for us."

I stood and he opened his arms and I rested my head on his chest. I sobbed and felt the tears on my cheeks. "Jeremy," I said.

His fingers gripped my arms and for a moment he held me to him; then he seemed to sag and his hands dropped away. I walked quickly across the trampled grass of the basketball court and around the side of the house.

When I was out of sight I ran. Jeremy, Jeremy, Jeremy, I repeated over and over. I came to the front gate and leaned on one of the pillars, my body shaking. From behind the house I heard the faint thump, thump, thump of the basketball.

# Chapter 20

I opened my eyes. The condominium was empty and unresponsive. Across the room the stereo sat silent. I bunched the pillow under my head. So long ago, I thought, so many years ago, and yet, and yet . . . they seemed so real, Jeremy, Charles, Don, Mrs. Allison, the major. I still saw them the way they were, as though they had been preserved in crystal.

I lived in Canterbury for only a single school year, nine months. Yet the Anne Medford who left Canterbury that June was very different from the one who had arrived the September before. It was as though I was fated to be born a second time, as though I had to sever the cord binding me to my youth. I was older when I left, but was I wiser? I don't know.

A few months ago, for the first time in a long while, I thought of Karl and found I had forgotten his last name. I went through the alphabet letter by letter, A, B, C, D, searching for a clue. None came. Karl belonged in the life of that other, younger Anne Medford.

How many nights have I lain awake searching through the dark attic of my mind for the meaning of those months in Canterbury? So many that I wonder if I haven't, over the years, changed my memories, altered an inflection here, shifted an occurrence there, given the woman I was in 1944 the feelings of an Anne Medford of a later time. Have I cut and shaped those few months to fit a pattern better to my liking? I don't know.

There is no question in my mind, however, about most of the facts. I sold the house at Canterbury, but not until the ice broke in the river and pale green buds showed on the trees. And not for forty thousand dollars, but for much less—much, much less. I accepted the first offer. Not once have I regretted selling the house.

I've never returned to Canterbury. Jean lives there

still—she married a local attorney the year after I left
and has raised four children in the village. Not only
does she live in Canterbury, she and her husband own
one of the new homes on the heights overlooking the
river where my house and the Blackstock house once
stood.

Jean says I wouldn't know the village if I came back.
The movie theater, after being closed for years, is an
auction gallery. Santoro's has been demolished to make
room for a bank. Quinlan's Service Station, the honor
roll, the Strause Apartments are gone. The ferry no
longer shuttles between Newburgh and Beacon—cars
now cross on a four-lane bridge. The school? The building is used for grades one through eight. The older students go to a central school a few miles away. The new
school, Jean writes, is proud of its math team.

The river and the mountains endure. As do my
memories.

I was wide awake now. I pushed the pillow aside
and got up to walk into the kitchen, where I filled the
kettle with water and put it on the stove to heat. A
car purred by on the street; the sound was loud, hopeful,
but then it faded into the distance. Did I hear a cry
from the sidewalk in front? When I opened the door
a white cat slipped by me and leaped onto his favorite
chair.

"MacArthur," I said, "you should be staying out all
night now." Yet I didn't have the heart to banish him.
How many MacArthurs had there been? I'd lost count.
Somehow all white cats became MacArthur.

Another car. No, he'll drive on, I told myself. But
the car entered our garage, the sound of the motor
reverberated through the apartment. I sighed, relieved,
admitting only then how worried I had been. I walked
back to the kitchen, set two cups on the counter and
put a spoonful of instant coffee in each. The kettle on
the stove whistled. I heard the door from the garage
open and close. I poured the boiling water into the cups.
Footsteps crossed the living room. His arm circled my

waist and he pulled me against him, pressed his lips to my hair.

"Sorry I'm so late," Don said. "You know what it's like after one of those meetings. We went over to the club and what with one thing and another . . ."

"It's all right," I said. "I just couldn't seem to sleep so I decided to have a cup of coffee. Want one?"

He nodded and sat on the stool across the counter from me. A bit heavier, I thought, hairline receding a little, a few more wrinkles in his face. But he looked so boyish when he smiled.

"Still Van Johnson," I said.

"What?"

"Van Johnson. You know I've always thought you looked like him."

Don grunted as he stirred cream and sugar into his coffee. "Swanson was at the meeting," he said. "Do you know what he wants to do now? Build the new Alta Vista school on the open plan. With hardly any windows because without rooms there won't be enough supports for the roof. With no windows the school will be a big cold barracks of a place. These young guys and their so-called modern ideas. They leap aboard every passing bandwagon."

"You knew he'd make changes when the board brought him in as superintendent."

"He should at least wait till he gets his feet wet. He isn't dry behind the ears yet! At first I thought we'd get along—he's likeable, no denying that—but now I'm not sure."

"Know who he sounds like?" I asked.

"No, who?" Don put his hand into the jar on the counter beside us.

"I ate the last cookie this afternoon," I told him.

"You're wrong, I've found one." He held the cookie up with a smile of triumph. "Tell me, who does Swanson remind you of?"

"Don Nevins," I said. "The Don Nevins of thirty years ago."

Don stopped with the cookie halfway to his mouth.

Frowning, he put down his cup and leaned back on the stool. Then he laughed, laughed until he had to wipe his eyes with his handkerchief. He reached out, took my chin between his fingers, bent forward and kissed me. "Anne," he said, "whatever would have become of me if I hadn't married you?"

"You'd probably be superintendent of schools instead of the assistant."

"No, I'd be just another stuffy cliché-ridden English teacher."

I shook my head. "No, never, not you," I said, but I thought with satisfaction there was more truth than poetry in what he said. Anne, I told myself, there you go again using one of his expressions. "Want your coffee warmed?" I asked. Don nodded and I brought the kettle from the stove and poured.

"I was a pretty darn good English teacher," Don said. "Fifteen years in the classroom before I went back for the credentials in administration."

"I know you were. Probably the reason I finally said yes."

"Remember the novel I was writing then, when I met you in Canterbury?" I nodded. "I took the manuscript out of the closet the other day and read it. Know what?"

"What?"

"It's terrible. Goes on and on without ever getting anyplace. All philosophy and no action. The characters aren't real. And once I thought I'd be a candidate for the Pulitzer Prize."

"You put a lot of good ideas in that book," I said. "A lot have come true."

"I've been working on it again." Don smiled sheepishly. "Down at the Education Center. Not making changes—I'm sort of starting from scratch."

"Don, that's wonderful. With the years you had as a teacher and now being in administration . . . "

"Yes, if you learn from experience at all I should have something to say now, about people and about education. No more philosophy, though; I'll just write about men and women who have ideas and problems and see what happens to them." He ate the last of the cookie. "Pretty good," he said. "The chocolate-chip cookie, I mean."

"Homemade."

Don looked into my eyes and for a moment I imagined we were sitting across from each other in Santoro's on the day we met, the day of the first faculty meeting. "I've never told you this," Don said, "about how I felt once when we were in Canterbury. I remember I came to your apartment to take you out, to a movie I suppose, and you walked down the front steps—it must have been a few months after you got out of the hospital, I remember how pale you were—and there was snow on both sides of the path and you had on your grey coat, the one with the fur collar."

"The fox fur," I said.

"Yes, the fox fur, and you smiled at me and you were so beautiful, your face reddening from the cold, and you wore a hat with a little veil. You were so lovely I hurt inside, actually hurt, just from looking at you."

My throat tightened and I felt tears come to my eyes. I put my hand over his on the counter. "Thank you," I said. "Thank you for telling me."

"Even this belatedly?"

"Even so. Maybe it means more to me now, like a surprise saved for just the right time."

"You want to know something crazy?" he asked. "Back then, that same time in Canterbury, for a while I had this notion, this foolish notion about that fellow, the strange dark one who shot his father. Jeremy? Yes, Jeremy Blackstock. I thought you sort of liked him. Wait, don't say anything, I know the idea is crazy, like I said. But I was jealous of him."

I pressed the back of his hand with my fingers.

"Funny," he said, "the way your imagination works overtime when you're young." Don got up and rinsed out the two cups and set them on the sink. "He died, didn't he? Jeremy? About ten years back?"

"Yes," I said, "he died." On the tenth of February, I thought.

"Only in his forties," Don said. "Makes you think. The Blackstocks, all dead, the mother, the father, the son. And Jeremy never married, did he?"

"No," I said, "he never married."

Don came to me and I slid from the stool. He held me lightly in his arms. "Tired?" he asked.

"Yes," I said, "but not that tired."

We went hand in hand to the bedroom, undressed and made love. Afterward we lay side by side, content.

"I wish we'd had children," I said.

"Ummmm." Don laced his fingers behind his head. "Yes, I suppose we shouldn't have given up so easily after you got sick that time."

"It's not too late. To adopt one I mean."

"Would they let us? At our age and all?"

"Yes, they've changed their rules a lot the last few years. I checked and we could."

"You're serious, aren't you? You're not just talking?"

"Yes. Serious, I mean."

"Let's sleep on it," he said. He turned over onto his side. "We'll talk the whole idea over tomorrow. O.K.?"

"O.K.," I said. I curled up next to him, knowing sleep would come. I smiled, thinking of having a child, thinking of Don and of our marriage. We had a good marriage, Don and I. With the years I had come to love him—just as I'd thought I would. As I'd hoped I would. I accepted the fact of our being together for the rest of our lives without question. I was happy.

Why, then, can I never seem to lay the past to rest? Will the memories come back to haunt me until the day I die? They don't return often—not every day, not even every week.

I may wake in the night, knowing I have dreamed of Canterbury, of the house overlooking the river, of the great rooms with the voices beckoning me from beyond.

Or I may be on the freeway with the dial of the car radio set at an all-music station when a band plays "Among My Souvenirs," and minutes later I rouse myself with a start, realizing I have no memory of driving the last five miles.

Or I may look into the sky on a clear night and see a star fall, making a silver arc across the blackness.

And when I do, I remember—I remember Canterbury, and I remember Jeremy.